W9-AIB-900

AND THE MEEK SHALL NOT INHERIT THE EARTH

" 'You can't do this,' Alec said, weakly.

'The spark,' Astor said, refusing to conceal his triumph. 'You wanted it—there it is.'

The vision vanished.

'Once the existence of this barbaric weapon becomes known—the location, by the way, is a jungle in Borneo—war will become inevitable. Our only problem is timing. We do not dare reveal this secret until the android army is prepared to take the field. Then, and only then, we can—'

'No!' Alec cried. 'The whole idea is inhuman.'

'Of course it is.' Astor laughed and looked deliberately around the table.

'Aren't we?' "

Inheritors of Earth

Gordon Eklund and
Poul Anderson

PYRAMID BOOKS NEW YORK

INHERITORS OF EARTH

A PYRAMID BOOK

Published by arrangement with Chilton Book Company

Pyramid edition published August 1976

This novel is based on the story "Incomplete Superman" by
Poul Anderson, copyright © 1950 by Columbia Publications,
Inc.

Printed in the United States of America

PYRAMID PUBLICATIONS
(Harcourt Brace Jovanovich)
757 Third Avenue, New York, N.Y. 10017

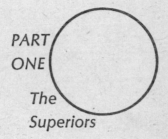

PART
ONE
The
Superiors

Happily humming one of the few really melodic popular tunes of the day, Alec Richmond rode the gently
moving walkway down the corridor toward his office
door. He was in such a good mood, so happy and con-
tented with the whole world and every soul in it, that
he felt almost shameful. But there was no way of
changing his attitude, not unless he somehow managed
to forget what had happened only a few hours earlier.
His employer, Theodore Mencken, had finally signed a
government contract both he and Alec had been stren-
uously laboring to land for six months or more. That
contract meant money—several hundred thousand new
dollars—but Alec knew the reason for his good mood
was not money alone. It was the power and success
and prestige that went with the contract and the fact
that his accomplishments nearly required his promotion
within the ranks of the Superiors. Alec didn't see how
Astor or any of the others could expect to keep him
out of the Inner Circle a day longer. Heretic or not, he
had done what he had set out to do. Weren't there few
others—very few—who could claim the same?

Nor was the contract the only excuse he had for
feeling pleased. Outside for an hour of lunch, he had
discovered a uniquely glorious spring day, bursting
with real sunshine, blue sky, fresh air, clean clouds. As
soon as he ironed out a few minor details with Ted
Mencken, he would be free to begin a month's vacation. He was really looking forward to that. The only
problem was that he wanted to go back east—to New
York—where he could confront the Inner Circle face-
to-face, while Anna said no. She thought the Inner
Circle—the Superiors who sat on it, at least—a dreadful bore. She said she wanted to go someplace else, to
Mexico or Central America or Free Brazil, anyplace
with real sunshine. Alec shook his head, wishing he

had time for play and sunshine. Maybe later—in a few years—when he was settled.

The office door was closer. Alec read the simple block letters printed in the air:

THEODORE MENCKEN
Agent

The walkway brought him to the brink of the office door. Bracing his knees to withstand the sudden cessation of velocity, Alec jumped off. He removed a key from his pocket and inserted it in the lock. He turned his hand.

The door opened without resistance.

Alec swore and stepped hastily inside. He had given Ted strict orders never to leave the front door unlatched. It didn't matter if he was inside or not. The door must always be locked.

Shutting the door, Alec took a step forward. As soon as he did, he knew that nothing was ever going to be the same again.

He felt Ted Mencken, and Ted Mencken was dying.

A wave of agony swept across Alec's mind and sent him down to his knees. He grabbed his head in his hands and screamed, trying to bite down on his tongue to shut off the cries. "Good God," he moaned, as wave after wave of suffering ran through his mind. He knew he was weeping like a baby with the secondhand agony he was forced to endure. "Ted, Ted, Ted," he whispered, unable to make himself heard. Mechanically, without thinking, his knees swiveled toward the door, but his muscles seemed frozen stiff—turned to ice by some dreadful magic—and he could not move an inch forward. "Ted, Ted," he whispered again. They had come. The others. Today of all days. They had come and got Ted.

He wanted to call out and tell Ted that he was coming. Bit by bit, he erected a tenuous shield around his mind, attempting to hold back as much of the agony as possible. At least he could think now. He managed to stop weeping but the desire to flee—to get out of this room and away from the pain and leave Ted to die—remained so powerful he had to waste precious energy trying to subdue it. At last, he began to crawl forward, moving on his hands and knees. He was glad the office was soundproof; at least he didn't have to worry about people, attracted by the sound of his own cries and Ted's, interrupting and finding him this way. But that had been a blessing for the others too, he realized. When they had come to do their dirty work, no one had interrupted them either; no one heard a sound.

But Ted heard. He was calling out now, his voice faint, more like an animal than a man, barely an indecipherable whisper. Crawling, Alec tried to reply:

"Ted ... hold on ... it's me—it's Alec ... I'm coming ... try to—"

A whimper rose in answer: "Alec, oh, Alec ... please ... please ..."

"I'm coming," Alec called. He tried to crawl faster. The office consisted of three identically sized rooms, each opening into the next. The farther he progressed, the more difficult it became to withstand the agony. When he entered the second room, he forced his fingers under his jacket and removed the revolver he kept holstered there. Pausing briefly, he flicked off the safety, then checked to ensure a bullet was resting in the proper chamber. Then he went forward, holding the gun ahead of him. Ted's agony continued to burn inside his mind. Outside, in the open world beyond, it was a simple process to prevent stray, unwanted thoughts and feelings from intruding into his own mind. But Ted was not simply thinking and feeling; he was dying. And there was no way Alec could prevent those awful thoughts from penetrating way down to the very core of his own being.

He made it. Finally. The door leading into the third room. The light was not burning. He was grateful to them for that. The last thing he needed now was to have to look at Ted Mencken as well as kill him. Feeling him was horrible enough—seeing might well force Alec past the precarious edge of madness. He crawled into the dark room. Stopping, he tried to

9

concentrate upon the source of the agony, attempting to discern its exact direction. His hand moved carefully, raising and lowering the revolver, gauging and estimating the shot. He didn't try to say a word. He thought Ted was silent too. Both knew this must be the end.

Alec fired. The gun exploded with a tremendous heaving sigh. Ted screamed. Alec dropped the gun, then fell forward, hurling his cheek against the cold bare floor. His body shook and trembled. His hands opened and closed spasmodically.

But it was over.

At last, slowly, he regained control of himself. His mind was free. His forehead throbbed with pain, as if struck by a powerful hammer, but a headache was nothing compared to what he had already been forced to endure. He tottered to his feet and staggered toward the nearest wall. He struck the resilient plastic a brutal blow. From above, soft light began to flicker into existence.

Theodore Mencken stood against the farthest wall. Alec saw the bullet hole in the man's chest. From the silence, he knew Ted was dead. There was no need to check for breath or pulse or heartbeat.

But the bullet—the damage it had done—was nothing compared to what had been done before. Alec could barely recognize the agonized, twisted features of his employer.

Why? he thought, searching desperately for some answer, some solution. Wasn't there any other way?

His mind finally comprehended what his eyes were seeing and he felt sick. Gagging, he turned and rushed out of the room. Halfway to the bathroom—set aside from the first room—he began to giggle. He couldn't stop himself. It seemed so funny. The monsters, he thought—the cold, heartless monsters. Why had they done it that way? Was it the cross that Ted, a devout Catholic, wore? Or was it the photograph of Ah Tran, the so-called new messiah, that decorated that same wall? Were they trying to make some statement? Was the horror merely some simple exercise in monstrous

10

irony? What kind of people could they be? How could they be so—so inhuman?

Like a three-dimensional tape sculpture suddenly materializing in the middle of the air, Alec saw that horrible sight again. Ted. Bent. Twisted. Dying. Nailed to the wall—spikes glinting in the light—blood surging from the wounds in his hands, feet, neck.

Theodore Mencken—agent—crucified.

The vision made him sick again. He reached the bathroom just in time and, once inside, he never wanted to leave.

two

It seemed to take hours before Alec finally managed to wrest a free seat on the transbay hovercraft but, almost as soon as he had, the craft set down in Oakland and waited there an hour because of essential military maneuvers being conducted in the area. He hung onto his seat, twitching with nervous impatience. An elderly woman sitting across the aisle tried to sound him out about the possibility of war but he refused to answer, pretending instead that she was directing her remarks to the small boy who sat beside him.

By the time he at last reached the terminal gate down the road from his home, it was well past midnight. Stepping into the clean air that remained from the day, he turned and silently regarded the view, a stream of directionless lights flickering upon the placid remnants of San Francisco Bay. His home was located high in the hills behind Berkeley. He turned away from the lights and trudged up the narrow gravel walk that led to his door. Along both sides of the path, stands of gnarled oak—twentieth century anachronisms—stretched toward and partly concealed the sky. A chilly wind whipped at his long hair. Crickets sang and an occasional mosquito buzzed.

Alec was oblivious to all this. Instead, his mind—capable of juggling a dozen or more separate lines of

11

thought—raced along a multitude of complex and interwoven paths. But even that many possible alternatives were not sufficient to contain the entirety of his thoughts tonight. Too many things had happened to him all at once. What could he do?

Reaching the door with shocking suddenness—no light shined upon the porch—he struggled to let himself in. But he had barely begun to twist the knob when the door popped open, revealing the chiseled features of Eathen. Alec stepped back. The last thing he needed to see tonight was this android. "Get out of my way."

"Yes, sir," Eathen said.

Alec brushed angrily past him, entering the living room. It was dark, silent, uninhabited. He turned on a heel and confronted Eathen, who had followed.

"Where is she?"

"In the garden, I believe."

"Are you sure?"

"Yes."

"What's she doing out there? It's nearly one o'clock."

"I wouldn't know, sir."

"No," Alec said, realizing the futility of insulting a creature that wasn't even human but unable—after today—to restrain himself. "No, I suppose you wouldn't."

"I'm sorry, sir."

For a moment, unable to choose, Alec stood rooted in the half-light, half-darkness between the living room and the corridor. The house was a vast structure—built some fifty years before—thirty rooms arranged in a doughnut square; a central garden a quarter-acre in size occupied the middle, the eye. They had moved in less than two months ago. Alec was attracted by the ostentation of the place, the sense of the past it contained, while Anna liked the idea of the garden. She knew the common and scientific names of every plant and flower out there.

"Stay here," he told Eathen, then set off down the corridor. A glass wall—transparent—the lighted garden showing beyond—rose to block his path. He stepped easily through the wall, his feet coming down upon moist dirt. Trees and bushes crowded around him. He sprang forward, finding a faintly visible path.

"Anna! I'm home! Are you here?"

He hadn't expected her to answer—nor did she—but he thought he knew where she would be. In the center of the garden a tiny creek emerged briefly from the earth, flowing for perhaps a dozen meters before sinking once more beneath the soil. A high arched bridge spanned the stream. He found Anna here, seated upon the crown of the bridge, her long legs dangling past the edge, eyes remotely fixed upon the ribbon of water below. Alec halted at the foot of the bridge and stood without speaking, preferring her to recognize him first. He glanced above, where a transparent dome sealed the garden off from the rest of the world and kept the often deadly fumes of the air from penetrating to infect the more exotic foliage. Dozens of tiny lights had been carefully arranged upon the surface of the glass to resemble the pattern of the nightly stars. There was a big yellow light too—a constantly full moon.

"Hello," Anna said, at last. But she did not look at him.

"I'm home," he said. A soft artificial wind filtered through the high branches of the nearby trees. Listening closely, he could hear the faint pulse of distant music.

"Is there something you want?"

"Yes," he said.

"What?"

Anna was three years younger than Alec—she was twenty-six—but looked far older. Her eyes were dark, her features firm and set, her skin a deep olive in color. She affected dark clothing—tonight she was dressed in a black, thigh-length jumpsuit with matching boots and gloves—and her hair, also black, streamed down past the small of her back. She wore a dark shade of lipstick and had painted wide black circles around both eyes. Now, turning to face him directly, the dark pit of

13

her mouth opened slightly; she seemed to be trying to smile.

He chose to tell her now. "Ted Mencken died today."

She shrugged one shoulder weakly, conveying—radiating—*So what?*

"They did it—the others. They came into the office and killed Ted."

Between Alec and Anna—the same as any Superiors—direct speech was superfluous. They communicated through the means of radiations: combinations of gestures, occasional half-spoken words, and, most importantly, emotions. As Alec stood awaiting her reply—if any—he clearly felt her coldness, her utter lack of feeling or compassion. If he hadn't known Anna—if he had not been aware of her ability to control and conceal her true feelings—if she had been some stranger vaguely met upon a public street—he knew he would have hated her.

"That's a pity," she expressed to him.

His anger flashed: "Is that all you can say?"

"What else? What do you expect me to do? Cry? I didn't know the man—he was only human."

"They crucified him. Nailed him to the wall and let him bleed to death. They—"

She laughed. "How ironic." Alec had told her before of Ted's devoutness, his interest in the Ah Tran movement.

"You don't seem to understand what this means to us. Without that contract, we're as poor as paupers. We'll have to move out of this house. We'll—"

"And you won't," she said, "get into your Inner Circle."

"No," he admitted. "I won't."

She sprang off the bridge, pushing herself boldly into the air. Her long body descended gracefully toward the ground. As a child, Anna had danced and those years of knowing how to channel the raw impulses of her body had never wholly left her. She landed in the dirt beside Alec and said, "Now we can go to Mexico."

14

He shook his head. "We can't go anywhere till this mess is straightened out."

"Let it work itself out."

He laughed. "Hardly. I've been ordered to stay."

"Ordered? You're kidding. By whom?"

He answered with real pleasure, having restrained the impulse until now: "By the police. By a certain Inspector Cargill."

"I've heard of him."

"He thinks I killed Ted."

"Oh, no," said Anna, but instead of shocked she seemed amused. "Come on." She took his arm casually. "Forget all that. There's something I want to show you."

"But—" He allowed her to lead him through the garden. Somewhere nearby, an invisible bird began to shriek. She knew exactly where she was taking him. Sometimes the higher branches of the trees would blot out the light from above but, even in total darkness, Anna neither faltered nor wavered. She already knew the garden as well as anyone could. She spent every possible waking moment out here. Even when she was working.

"Here," she said, pretending to be unaware of his surface thoughts. (He had intended that she would hear.) "Duck down." They slipped underneath a garland arch, stooping. On the other side was a small sheltered area, devoid of trees or other foliage. A pair of armless wooden benches faced each other. Anna and Alec assumed opposing seats. They waited. The bird continued to shriek.

At last, Alec said, "What is this all about?"

"A little surprise. I've rigged this area for sensotape. A live show is running tonight. Ah Tran will be entering Tokyo at two our time."

"Are you trying to be funny? You know that—"

"Ted Mencken?" She clicked her tongue. "I told you to forget him, Alec."

"I can hardly do that." He felt himself growing angry again. "We have to discuss this. Besides everything else, you have to realize they killed Ted. They broke

15

into the office—in spite of all the precautions I took—
and they killed him. It could have just as easily been
me, Anna."

"It wasn't," she said, as if this were a question under
dispute.

"Of course it wasn't."

"Then what are you worried about? Call Astor.
Have him help you. While I'm watching the messiah,
you call."

"You're supposed to be my wife."

"I am. But—call."

"No, I'll watch too."

"Have it your own way," she said, settling back,
shutting off her mind from his gaze.

He leaned back too, suddenly exhausted now,
drained by the spiraling tension of the day. He could
have fallen asleep but, a bare instant later, the sensotape began, forcing him to be alert again. All at once,
he couldn't see Anna any more; the garden had disappeared. Instead, he was sitting—upon the bench—in
the middle of a wide, straight, concrete boulevard.
High, rectangular, glass-and-steel buildings rose along
both sides of the street like crazed freaks of mecha-
nized nature. A huge mob had gathered here, occupying both sidewalks—small, sturdy, sharp-eyed faces—
Japanese. The street was strangely bare of traffic. A
scattering of policemen scurried across the boulevard,
shouting directions at the passive mob. A mass of
whispering voices, fused together in a single murmur,
spoke of general anticipation, but there was barely a
hint of impatience and none of anger. Alec followed
the crowd's collective stare, gazing far down the avenue. The air was thick with industrial fumes; Tokyo
was still the most poisoned major city on Earth. He
could clearly smell the ugly stink. Somewhere—unseen—a brass band played poorly. The tune was one
of Ah Tran's own compositions—a new hymn. Alec
had been too busy the past few months to take much
notice of this new cult. Ted had occasionally mentioned Ah Tran to him but never gone into details. As
far as Alec was concerned, prophets and messiahs

16

came and went; the Inner Circle endured. It was the latter that demanded the whole of his attention.

Silence. The band ceased playing. The crowd held its breath. Alec leaned forward on the edge of the bench, intrigued in spite of himself, leg muscles tense, throat dry. The atmosphere of eager anticipation was infectious.

Now, at the far end of the boulevard, a dim object materialized—a faint pinprick of motion. The object slowly grew. Soon, it was identifiable as an automobile—an old roofless model—a convertible. He could even hear the rumbling roar of the old piston engine. One man drove while another stood upon the rear seat. This man, as the automobile rolled forward, swung back and forth like a pendulum, bowing and waving at the severed portions of the crowd. Ah Tran. Yes—it had to be. The crowd's response was muted, strangely meager. Only a few waved. None cheered or shouted or applauded. Once the car had passed, most turned silently and went away.

As the procession came steadily forward, Alec expected the scene to change. At any moment, he expected to find himself in another place—perhaps floating in the air—dangling above the crowd. But he remained where he was: in the middle of the street. The car came closer, so close now that he could easily make out the scratches and dents in the hood and fenders. Were they going to make him remain here to be run over and crushed beneath these tons of rumbling steel? What sort of amateur production was this? Hadn't Anna said this was a network presentation? What could be wrong? The car was nearly on top of him now. He found it impossible to convince himself of the difference between reality—which this wasn't, could not be—and sheer illusion. He tried to gain his feet. He wanted to run away. His shoes were glued to the concrete. He tried to shout, threw a hand in front of his eyes, screamed, cried out. The chrome bumper gleamed inches away. *No, no, no!*

The car stopped. If he had wished—if it had been at

all possible—he could have reached out and touched the warm steel.

A door slammed. He heard footsteps—soft, pattering bare feet. He was bathed in cold sweat.

Then Ah Tran appeared. A small man, barely five feet, dressed in a black hoodless cowl. Very dark, wrinkled skin—a bald smooth skull. He could have been any kind of man, any race.

He stopped before the bench and bowed to Alec. His lips moved, forming words. The actual sound seemed removed in time from the mechanical gesture: "How are you?"

"Fine," Alec lied, too startled for anything else.

"Then," said Ah Tran, "I have something for you. A gift."

"But—" Alec began, hoarsely.

Ah Tran sternly waved him silent. Smiling ambiguously, he reached around his neck and removed a gold medallion the size and shape of a large eye. Handling the object with extreme care—as if it were fragile—he passed it over to Alec. "I was told to offer this to you," Ah Tran said.

"Told?" Alec asked. A part of him insisted that all of this was impossible, it could not be happening, that he was in reality thousands of miles from this place. But the medallion looked and felt real; he could see Ah Tran as clearly as day. His mind would not accept these protests.

Ah Tran slowly raised a hand. "Please—no questions."

"But—"

Again, the uncertain smile. "Please." Turning suddenly, Ah Tran headed back toward the car, slipping quickly around the side and disappearing from view. Alec heard a door slam. The engine began to cough.

He ignored these extraneous sensations and peered down at the medallion. Inscribed upon the upturned face was the profile of a man, carefully detailed, shaded. Alec studied this picture intently and recognition dawned slowly.

The face was his own.

18

He turned the medallion over, expecting to find an explanation here, but the second side was smooth, blank. Puzzled, he turned back to the face and held the medallion between his thumb and forefinger, moving it against the dim evening sunlight.

There were words printed here. A small grouping of block letters above the top of his own face. He struggled to read the inscription. THE MEEK, it said. He blinked, seeing THE MEEK SHALL INHERIT THE EARTH.

That was all. That single, brief, utterly banal slogan. What was the idea? Whose joke was this? Whose lie? It was not the meek who were fated to prevail, it was the strong, the powerful, the superior. That was nature's unchangeable law. Burning with frustration and rage, Alec thrust the medallion deep in his fist, threw back his arm and hurled it high above the crowd.

The moment the medallion faded from view—a tiny dot against the blank gray sky—the scene was gone. He was back in the garden again. Anna sat across from him, slumped down, face hidden in her hands. He jumped to his feet, pointed a finger, and cried: "You! You did that! What was the idea?"

He loomed above her, knowing she would soon raise her eyes and laugh in his face. A petty laugh, triumphant. But she said nothing, did not move. Suddenly, her face turned up. Their eyes met. He saw something in her expression, a thing painful and haunting, that caused his anger to recede.

"What is it?" he asked, abruptly concerned.

She shook her head, sadly at first, then faster, faster, until her long hair lashed at her cheeks. She leaped at him. Before he could protect himself, her long fingernails slashed down, raking his face. He screamed, reached out, grabbed her wrists. As usual, her strength was enormous. Her feet stamped on his. Howling, he danced back, refusing to release her wrists. There was blood on his face. Anna spit at his eyes. "Eathen!" he cried, hoping the android was lurking near. "Eathen—hurry—the garden!"

Anna was shouting too, drowning his cries. It was

not help she wanted. He tried to understand what she was saying. Suddenly, she relaxed, nearly falling, dangling in his grip, as limp as death. Her eyes went shut.

"What did you see?" he whispered. "Tell me what."

Her eyes opened. She grinned. "You!" she cried. "I saw you!"

"What?" He shook her. "What do you mean? Tell me!"

She broke loose, springing away, landing on the balls of her feet like a jungle cat—a panther. She spun away, seeking escape, but just as she did, Eathen emerged from the bushes behind. He held a hypodermic needle in his hand. In a fluid practiced motion, he stepped forward and grabbed Anna. Unconcerned with her clawing fingers and snapping teeth, he drove the needle deep into her bare thigh. She groaned, cried out, then went limp and lifeless.

Eathen held her up.

"It's about time," Alec said. "Where were you?" He dropped back to the bench and wiped at the blood on his face.

"I had to mix the potion," Eathen explained.

"Well, take her inside," Alec said. "Put her to bed. I have to leave early tomorrow."

Eathen nodded and picked Anna up, holding her as though she were a child and he her father. "Will you wish me to wake you, sir?"

"That won't be necessary." He did not expect to be sleeping tonight. "Just go away and leave me alone."

"Yes, sir," said Eathen.

three

Through the transparent wall of his study, Alec Richmond was allowed a serene view of the central garden. A fat bush—carefully stripped of thorns—it was a white rose, he thought—was centered behind the glass; it succeeded in interrupting but not in any way desecrating the natural view. He often came here to the study late at night to sit and work and think and watch. The garden rarely moved him when he was actually out in it, but at a greater distance the bright foliage did produce an attitude of stately beneficence, a collective tranquility, which was both relaxing and—as far as work was concerned—inspirational. He had completed the android designs in this very room. Eathen—the fruit of his work—had been presented to him here. He had been working here last night when Ted Mencken called to say that General Hopkins had agreed to issue a contract. Success, he recalled. That was what he had told Ted: we are now successful.

That recollection made him smile. The truth was that success now seemed the most hollow of words. What did it mean? In the garden nothing could be seen—not even shadows—for the real moon and stars were hidden by the dome and the artificial lights had been extinguished. Even the white rose—naked without its thorns—could barely be seen. He turned his chair away from the wall. Now he sat facing another wall lined with tapes and books, technical works concerning every known field of human science, a handful of histories and biographies, perhaps a dozen novels. Four of the novels—old frail paperbacks smelling of dust and age—sat on a small table beside his elbow. During the past hour, he had read all four, moving mechanically from one to the next. The words had drifted weakly through his mind. Each refused to connect with the one following; concepts had emerged abstract but senseless. He knew he needed something stronger than any book. Liquor? Drugs? He used neither. All that was left to him was himself: poor, frail Superior. He concentrated his attention there.

He could read a book as fast as the pages could be turned. He could feel another man's radiated emotions as if such qualities were bright signs printed for any person to read. He could do higher mathematics with a speed approaching that attained by more primitive computers. It was true: he could do this and that and the other. And, why not? He was Alec Richmond—a Superior. But what was the use? The point? Where did

21

all of these talents lead? His greatest accomplishment so far was producing a flesh-and-blood machine capable of committing legal murder with speed and precision. His employer was dead. His wife verged on sheer looniness. And himself? All he could do was sit alone in a dark room and feel sorry for himself.

This was more of the same. Self-pity: the most common of human frailties next to jealousy. Well, sometimes he felt jealous too, and there was no purpose served by being ashamed of these bare reactions. If he was indeed a little bit human, maybe he ought to admit it. Self-pity? Well, there were good reasons.

Years before, the Inner Circle had chosen to reject the term superman in favor of Superior (always capitalized). A superman, it was said, and Alec never quite understood this, conjured up visions of an overly muscled creature dressed in brightly colored long underwear. But—in spite of that—whatever it meant—he thought it was the more proper term. They were superior, yes, but many extraordinary men were that too. They were supermen, a new race, as far removed from simple *Homo sapiens* as that form of life had exceeded the ape.

But we pay the price, he thought. We are a tiny minority submerged within a vast majority. We are alone, fearful, paranoid. Our very existence is a deep, dark secret.

And that was without even mentioning the key factor, that supreme point around which all their existence necessarily revolved.

We are supermen, Alec thought, but we are incomplete supermen.

Was it a sign, a curse, a price? Perhaps it had to be that way. He could dimly recall, as a young boy, only faintly aware of his own painful heritage, reading an old novel about superior mutants. What had it been? In the book? Long tendrils—that was it—growing out of the skull of each mutant. That had been their sign. Well, the Superiors suffered from no such outward manifestation. By and large, they were handsome and healthy but otherwise no different from any human.

22

Their sign—their curse—the price they paid for superiority—lay deep inside.

It was called sterility.

In all of recorded time—since the first two Superiors had met nearly a half-century past—no child (not one) had been born to them. The Inner Circle said this would pass in time. They were very optimistic about the situation. But—as with other official positions—Alec was skeptical. The Inner Circle said, *We must wait until our race has matured, then we shall flood the earth with our children.* Alec smiled. It wasn't maturity—it was fate.

Nor was that all. There was reversion to consider too. Anna suffered from this but she was not alone. Fits of madness. Irrationality. Insanity. Crimes perpetrated. Murder. Suicide. Why? If they were superior, why couldn't they at least control their baser instincts?

Alec remembered how the Inner Circle had once distributed a list of various famous people who had died childless. Alec, without amusement, had protested the project; he suggested a second, contrary listing; all of those men and women throughout history who had committed mass murder, who had died in asylums, who had been burned as witches. These were just as likely to be historical Superiors as all the great childless men and women whose names could be discovered.

But they would not admit that. His protest had gone unanswered. The Inner Circle—under Astor's direction—had a simple solution for everything, even madness. Reversion was exactly what the term implied. Since Superiors were supermen who had not quite yet achieved maturity, then ugly vestiges of humanity undoubtedly lingered on. It was this buried curse that rose up and usurped the careful functioning of the Superior mind. It took control. Madness—murder—suicide. This was another price to be paid, but once maturity was attained—that same distant goal again—then real inward peace would reign.

Or consider the case of the others—the ones who had murdered Ted Mencken. The Inner Circle position concerning the existence of the others was sheer wish-fulfillment fantasy. For years—ever since the Superiors had first discovered each other—they had been plagued by a series of inexplicable incidents. Strange accidents. Vicious murders—like Ted's. It soon became clear that someone—or something—was behind all this. Who? What? Men who had somehow stumbled upon the secret of the Superiors and were determined to crush them? Was it the government, acting officially but in secret? Or was it something worse—uglier—something alien? The Inner Circle made no effort to answer these questions. When Astor heard about Ted, he would no doubt react as he always did, shaking his head and saying what a horrible thing it was. But the others? Astor would laugh. That was pure myth—a horror story—there was no such thing. The accidents, incidents, murders? Sheer coincidence, nothing more.

Sheer stupidity, Alec thought, nothing more. But Astor and the Circle were scared. He couldn't blame them. Thinking of Ted, he was scared too.

Then he heard a scream.

He stopped dead and stood up.

The scream came again.

Oh. He sat back down. Only Anna. She often awoke like this—driven from a drugged sleep by unseen demons she would never describe.

She screamed again.

This time he moved. Where was Eathen? He stepped into the corridor with deliberate lack of haste. Anna's room was close by. She was still screaming, her shrill terror penetrated his defenses, causing him to walk faster than he wished.

When he reached the bedroom door, it stood open. He remained in the corridor and peered inside. The room was very dark. He could sense her radiated fear but it was softer now, more subdued. He thought he could hear a voice.

Suddenly, Eathen filled the doorway.

Alec made a move to enter the room but Eathen reached out with a wide arm and blocked his way.

"She is sleeping," he said.

"She wasn't a minute ago," Alec glared at the arm in front of him. "Get out of my way."

"She said she didn't want you."

"She said that?"

"Yes, sir," Eathen replied, coldly. "She dreamed about you and didn't want to see you."

"But she's sleeping now." Alec fought to maintain his dignity in front of the android. But he couldn't help hating them—Anna and Eathen—his wife and son. "Are you sure? She won't wake up again?"

"She is resting peaceably now."

Alec confirmed this observation. He sensed Anna. She was radiating a strong contentment now, a sense of peace.

"All right," he said, turning away from the dark room. "Go back in and stay with her."

"I intend to, sir." But Eathen did not move.

"Then do it," Alec said.

"Yes, sir."

But still Eathen did not vacate his position at the doorway until Alec's dim footsteps had disappeared down the soft, carpeted hallway.

four

His preconceptions shattered, Alec Richmond sat, turning his thumbs with mild impatience. He would have preferred getting out of here—was bored by the waiting—and yet it was, he had to admit, completely different from what he had expected.

Before coming here, if asked, he would have imagined the offices occupied by the Homicide Division of the San Francisco Police Department as an ugly, dreary place—a dirty, stained floor—battered, torn furniture—inhabited by dim, lumbering men engaged in squalid combat with an even drearier bunch of alleged murderers. Not that there were many of these. Crimes of passion tended to flourish during times of societal stress and change. An atmosphere of uncertainty—almost one of ambiguity—a lack of firm bearings had to exist before the average man could be plunged into that most passionate of crimes: murder. But, for the last few decades, American society had been a paragon of stability. Only the handful of remaining outcasts, a few thieves, pimps, prostitutes, or con-men, had a chance to experience those base emotions necessary as a prelude to murder. Alec had seen all the available statistics; more importantly, he had his talent—he knew what people were feeling when he passed them on the street. The average man—or woman—simply did not care enough about anything to kill.

Where his preconceptions had most been violated, however, was not in the polished floors or the bright walls or the plush furniture but in the people. Here he sat—like a child in a government home—surrounded by women.

The real detectives—Cargill and his helpers—were still hidden from him; this room was only the reception room. Still, it was all he had to go on. The most obvious of his companions was the receptionist herself—a sharp-eyed redhead, perhaps thirty, who manned her desk like an army defending a choice hunk of battlefield. Her strongest feelings—those he could hardly avoid—were concerned with a certain young man. He could not read her thoughts. That was an impossibility. Thoughts—except at the most conscious level—were not contained in words. They could not be seen and read line-by-line like the pages of a book. Thoughts erupted at random, bursting forth like the rays of the sun, without conscious dictation or direction; wholly separate conceptions frequently existed simultaneously. It was not a tidy process. The best a Superior could expect to know was the general aura—the atmosphere—of any given mind. To probe any deeper, interpretation was required.

Alec deciphered the maelstrom of the woman's feelings to mean that she had once loved a man. For reasons he could not expect to discover, they had recently separated. Because no one else had appeared to assume this man's place in her life, he remained a dominant presence in her mind. Alec—it was his greatest weakness—could not help feeling sorry for her. After all, in spite of the fact that she was merely human, her situation was not greatly different from his with Anna. Perhaps they should get together and compare sad notes. He briefly considered a direct approach, stepping forward and asking her to lunch. Ah, but what would the Inner Circle think? They would know, as they seemed to know everything. Fraternization with the enemy. In times past, when Superiors were relatively few and disorganized, even intermarriage between the two species had occurred. But such relations—even the most tenuous—were strictly forbidden today. Too dangerous—and demeaning. After all, would any normal man be interested in taking a female gorilla to lunch?

Besides which, the woman was really too simple for him. He was considerably more intrigued by the second woman in the room. She was somewhat younger than the other—probably about Anna's age—and much better looking, even beautiful, blonde, almost unearthly pale. Her thoughts and feelings radiated with such strength and power that it was difficult to avoid being swept under. Worse yet, her feelings were so strong that he could not decipher or interpret them. There was a deep, tremendous sadness there. Over what, or because of what, he couldn't begin to guess: the emotion itself was so vital that she failed to concentrate upon the subject itself. But he felt no pity for her. In spite of the bleakness of her emotions, an underpinning of undiluted strength of will remained firmly intact. This was a woman capable of taking on the whole world and its problems without faltering a step.

He tried to make a guess as to the cause of her grief. A boyfriend or husband? Considering where they were, perhaps he had been arrested. But this explanation seemed far too banal to explain the woman. Perhaps he was failing to meet the matter directly. There was no reason to implicate a man—the woman herself might be the criminal. He himself was suspected of a minor murder—why not she as well? She had killed the boyfriend or husband. She was a little bit sorry now, and yet he had got what he had coming too. So she was both glad and sorry and maybe somewhat concerned with her own safety—the police might catch her and they might not.

Hey, now, he wanted to say. *Don't let that worry you. I won't let them get you. When they ask, you tell them you spent the time of the murder in my company. A perfect alibi. We shared lunch in a mysterious little North Beach restaurant. We walked along the beach, watching the soiled waves. We—*

"Alec Richmond."

"Oh." He looked up, glimpsing—half-hidden behind the receptionist and her desk—a small, round man dressed in black billowing burlap. "I'm Richmond."

"Splendid." The man crooked a finger. "Inspector Cargill—remember me?"

Alec stood up, irritated that this conversation was taking place in front of the woman. He glanced over at her, and she was watching, wide-eyed and interested. Her radiated feelings told him nothing. "We only spoke on the phone."

"Of course." The finger went past his shoulder. "This way, please."

Alec nodded and quickly followed the round man through a door behind the receptionist. Back here, the dirty floors and dim detectives remained hidden. They followed a long, narrow corridor, quite empty of life, to its end. Cargill opened a door and ushered Alec into a tiny, cluttered room. A massive steel desk occupied nearly the whole of the cubicle, piled high with scattered papers. Alec searched for a chair and finally discovered one in front of the desk. Cargill scurried around behind and sat down, his head nearly hidden from view.

"Go ahead and sit," he told Alec. "Just dump that stuff on the floor."

Alec removed a three-foot stack of papers from the chair and then sat down.

"What do you want here?" Cargill asked.

"I believe you asked to see me."

"I did?" Cargill asked, his brow wrinkling in puzzlement.

"Why, yes—yes, you told me—"

"Ah." Cargill raised a finger toward the ceiling. "Of course—the body."

"What?" Alec wasn't receiving a thing from Cargill. The man seemed totally in control of his thoughts and feelings—he let nothing out beyond the most casual, surface thoughts. It was a mind that ran in strict, straight channels. This fact only added to Alec's disconcertment. It couldn't be deliberate. Could it?

"Identification. I want you to take a look at the body."

"Oh," Alec said, "you mean Ted's."

"You know?"

"Know what?"

"Whose body I'm going to show you."

"I naturally assumed—"

"And if you'd been wrong?"

"I . . ." Alec stopped, growing angry. "Look here, if you're trying—"

"Who killed him?"

"What?"

"Do you know?"

"If I did—"

"Was it you?" As he spoke, Cargill leaned farther and farther forward. Now he seemed almost prone upon the desktop, like a bird preparing for immediate flight.

"No," Alec said. "I certainly didn't—"

"Why not?" Cargill said, continuing to move.

"Because I had no reason. Ted was my boss, my friend. I wouldn't—"

"You're sure?" Cargill threw himself back, rebounding off his chair. Both hands waved wildly in the air. "Would you be willing to undergo truth tests?"

"Certainly," Alec said, smiling almost smugly. No test or device had yet been devised capable of detecting a Superior's lie. If Cargill meant to upset him, he was going about it the wrong way.

Cargill slumped down in his chair, plainly dejected,

29

his mind no more revealing than ever. He shook his head sadly, slowly, to himself.

Alec leaned forward, awaiting the next assault.

It came with a sudden blast. Cargill sat up, pointed straight at Alec's heart, demanded: "How many children?"

Alec lunged back. "None," he said. "I mean, none yet."

"Your authorization?"

"Three. But what does this have—?"

"Your wife have any children? Previous marriages?"

"No. But I'd like to know why—"

"Hush," said Cargill. He made a note on a stray sheet of paper, then looked up. "Two nights ago I saw one of your wife's sculptures. I don't mind saying it was a dazzling piece."

"Which one was it?" Alec asked, welcoming the new subject although he rarely took much interest in Anna's work.

"*Crime,*" said Cargill, triumphantly, "*and Punishment.*"

"Very funny," Alec said, unamused.

"Ah, no—a tragedy." Cargill begun to shuffle the papers nearest to him. The motion attracted Alec's gaze. Among the blank white sheets, he suddenly spotted a photograph. The face was very familiar: Ah Tran. Cargill raised the picture in his hands and studied it, looking from the smooth surface to Alec's face, then back again. "Do you know a man named Samuel Astor?" he asked.

"What?" Alec struggled to conceal his shock. How could Cargill know about Astor and the Inner Circle? He couldn't—it had to be impossible.

But Cargill repeated the name calmly and carefully: "Samuel Astor. Of New York."

Alec decided to risk a lie: "I don't believe I know him."

"Then that's funny," Cargill said, without explanation. He was shuffling papers again; the photograph of Ah Tran disappeared. He lifted a page and began to recite: "You and the deceased, Theodore Mencken,

30

worked together in a small firm. Mr. Mencken handled the business end while you were in charge of research. Much of your actual work was contracted out." His eyes appeared over the page. "What was the work?"

"I can't tell you," Alec said. "It was a matter of exceptionally high security."

"Androids," Cargill said—it wasn't a question.

"But—"

Cargill flashed a red, high security badge. "General Hopkins has already spoken to me. Obviously, this case intrigued him. Spies, you know. I was able to assure him espionage was not involved."

"Do you know that?" Alec asked.

"Oh, yes." Cargill smiled, almost diffidently. "I am, you realize, a police inspector."

"I know."

"Yes." He stood up and clasped his hands in front of him, cracking the knuckles with an ugly sound. "Then shall we get on with it? The body?"

"That's all?" Alec said. He couldn't believe it.

"For now." Cargill smiled reassuringly and stepped around the desk. He laid a kind hand on Alec's shoulder. "Though there is another thing that puzzles me. Where did you go to school?"

"A government home," Alec said, squirming away from the hand. He managed to gain his feet, looming above the tiny detective.

"Your parents?"

"I never knew either of them."

"Dead?"

"My mother, yes. My father—" he shrugged "—I don't know."

"Interesting," Cargill said, noncommittally.

"Why do you ask?"

"Curious." Cargill pointed at the door. "Shall we go?"

"Yes," Alec said. "Yes—of course." He hurried toward the door. These questions—his parentage, children—frightened him. They struck too close to the real truth. He would have to tell Astor. But Cargill knew about him too. What could it mean?

He dropped the thoughts as Cargill fled down the corridor. Halfway down its length, Cargill swerved pace. They entered the reception room together, interrupting the receptionist, who had been painting her knuckles a ghastly shade of green. The other woman—the sad one—still sat on the couch. Cargill, barely pausing, waved at her:

"Come along, please."

She stood up and followed Cargill and Alec into the corridor. Halfway down its length, Cargill swerved aside and slapped the left wall with his open hand. A pair of doors suddenly opened, revealing a concealed elevator. The three of them hurried inside. As the elevator descended, Cargill pointed at the woman, then at Alec:

"Alec Richmond," he announced, "and Sylvia Mencken."

"You're his daughter," Alec said. So that was the reason for her grief. He nearly smiled.

"How do you do?" she said, in a cool voice totally at odds with her inner turmoil and pain.

"All right," Alec said. What else? "And you?" He felt absurd as soon as the question left his lips.

She laughed wistfully. "Oh, fine." She smiled. "Under the circumstances."

The elevator, having descended to the lowest conceivable level, opened. The corridor down here glowed with a stark, unearthly light. Alec and Cargill walked together, while Sylvia Mencken trailed behind.

"This is the place," Alec said, "where you keep them."

"Yes—in here."

They turned into a large gray room. A big pink man abruptly materialized in front of them, waddling very close. He shook hands with each of his guests, bowing deeply from the waist while greeting Sylvia.

When the ceremonies were complete, the pink man scowled at Cargill. "Which one?" he asked.

"Seven-six-eight-three-nine," said Cargill.

"Ah, that fellow." The pink man nodded sharply. "A rather fascinating carcass." He smiled self-consciously, then bustled hastily away. Cargill indicated they should follow. Set in one wall, occupying the entirety of its length, was a series of metal drawers, like a monstrous file cabinet. The pink man went instinctively to one and drew it open. Alec followed Cargill over. They looked down together. There, lying upon a hard metal slab, as naked as could be, was Ted Mencken. He did not appear greatly changed from the last time Alec had seen him. The blood was gone, though.

"Well?" said Cargill.

Alec struggled to reply, but the ferocity of Sylvia's reaction—communicated through her involuntary radiations—drained his own. He barely managed to nod. "Yes," he said. "Yes, that's dead."

"Dead?" Cargill asked. "Did you say dead?"

"I meant Ted," Alec said.

The pink man was giggling at the slip. Alec could have crushed his ugly fat face with a rock.

"And?" Cargill said, wheeling to face Sylvia. "What have you got to say, my dear?"

His lines spoken, Alec allowed himself to be swallowed up within the girl's radiations. He was now finally able to understand her attitude of wistful regret. Seeing her dead father had made her recall, in disorganized mass, the many past times they had been together. Memories reached Alec in vague procession. He could tell that they had not always gotten along. In fact, often they had not. Sylvia was sorry. Yes, that was it. Now she understood that it was too late for everything that had not already occurred.

"It's my father," she suddenly said.

"Theodore Mencken?"

"Of course," she said, no longer facing the corpse.

"Shut it up," Cargill ordered the pink man.

The file drawer clanged shut. Alec opened his eyes and suddenly laid a hand on Sylvia's arm. "Let's get out of here," he said.

She smiled appreciatively and let him lead her out. Cargill came after. In the corridor, Sylvia drew away and leaned against the wall.

"Are you all right now?" Alec asked.

33

"Better," she said.

"Then I—"

Cargill stepped between them, cutting Alec off. He suddenly began to speak, but it was several moments before Alec was able to understand his words: ". . . many motives. I am speaking, of course, of years past. Men were even known—I can show you records that testify to this—known to kill during fits of sudden passion. Husbands would kill their own wives, fathers, their sons and daughters, vice versa, versa vice, ad infinitum. Some say those were horrible, horrible times. I wonder. Except for a brief period on the beat—a patrolman in the North Beach sector—I have devoted my adult life to detective work. I am head of this city's homicide squad. I am, in point of fact, that squad. Last year, I investigated four murders—two turned out to be accidents and one was a suicide. And the other? The few we do get year in and year out? I can assure you passion no longer plays a significant role in these crimes. What does?" He was staring hard at Alec, presumably expecting some response. But Alec had nothing to say. Sylvia seemed to be holding herself up only with the assistance of the wall. But Cargill went on: "I'll tell you what it is: power. That's the word I want. Murder nowadays is primarily a means of expressing power. I am stronger—greater—than you. You demur. In proof, I take your life. Well, I'll tell you." His voice rose passionately, filling the tiny corridor. Alec reached past him and grabbed Sylvia's arm. She had nearly fainted. "I want the old days back," Cargill said. "I want human murders for human motives. These crimes" (he waved back toward the morgue) "make me ill. We are all humans. We share this planet together. None is greater, more powerful, than another. I will—I promise you this—I will discover the perpetrator of this crime and guarantee that he is brought to justice. I will" (he was pointing at Alec now, his finger trembling with passion) "succeed in the way I always have and that man" (he turned to Sylvia) "or woman will be shown that the egotism that made him—or her—feel that murder was justified is a crime in itself

34

of the deepest and most dreadful sort. I promise you that much and" (his finger was back at Alec's belly) "and no more."

"Are you accusing me?" Alec said, glaring down at the finger.

"Of course not," Cargill said, dropping his hand.

"Then get out of my way. Can't you see that she's sick?"

"You may go now," Cargill said, and he turned off toward the elevator.

Alec held Sylvia by both her shoulders. His face was very close to hers. "Are you going to be all right? He's gone now."

"Yes," she said, barely managing to whisper. But he felt her gain more control of her body. She stood up, not attempting to draw away from him. "Will you take me out of here?"

"Of course." He helped her toward the elevator. It was gone now—carrying Cargill above. "I'll be glad to." He could feel the depth of her regard, her need for someone—anyone—him—who could help. "Of course I will."

"That man was horrible," she said.

"Yes. He thinks I killed your father. He was warning me."

They stopped beside the wall. Her face was less pale—she seemed able to stand unassisted now. She gazed at Alec.

"Did you?" she asked.

five

"I'd be glad to see you home," Alec said, as he and Sylvia Mencken descended the high concrete steps of the Hall of Justice.

"I don't want to go there—not yet."

"Well—where?"

"I think I'll just go over to the park and walk around."

35

"I really don't know if—"

She laughed. "You don't have to go." They paused at the edge of a moving walkway. This was not a busy part of town. An occasional passenger drifted past at a steady five-miles-per-hour. "But I would like to talk to you."

"Oh, I don't mind." He had been eager to get home to Anna. All that had occurred last night still seemed disturbing to him.

"Good," Sylvia said. She pointed across the walkway. "Go get us a cab."

Alec nodded, any thought of refusing now forgotten, and skipped across the walkway. He spoke quickly to a hovercab driver, then came back and fetched Sylvia.

Once the cab was airborne in the direction of Golden Gate Park, the driver asked Alec: "Any particular place in the park?"

Sylvia said, "Strawberry Hill."

"The top of the hill or beside the lake?"

"The lake. We can climb."

Alec rarely visited the park on his own. Even Anna did not care for it. The existence of so much raw nature in the midst of the concrete city seemed somehow improper—artificial—filled with conflict.

But, this time, as soon as he and Sylvia left the cab, he relaxed. It was another gorgeous day. A west wind, floating off the ocean, blew smooth and mild. Sylvia's feelings, as they reached him, were equally serene. He guessed she came here often.

The lake where they had set down was a wide moat encircling a high, tree-studded hill. A fleet of electric runabouts gently stirred the waters. Sylvia, in silence, led Alec over a wooden bridge to the edge of the hill. A dirt road ran here, sloping upward as it circled the hill. "I like walking here," she said. "The hill and trees on one side—the boats and water on the other."

He nodded in agreement. They moved up the dirt road. A bird, perched high in a tree, shrieked as they passed beneath. Alec shivered, reminded of the night before.

At last Sylvia spoke: "I imagine I owe you an apology."

"Oh, no," he said.

"But I did ask if you had killed Father."

"There's nothing wrong in asking that." A cluster of camera-laden tourists passed them. Alec felt their eyes. He was proud of himself, walking with such a beautiful woman. "Cargill thinks I did it. Why shouldn't you?"

"Cargill?" She smiled and touched his hand reassuringly. "What makes you think that?"

"The questions he asked me. That speech he made."

"Oh, that was nothing. He doesn't suspect you."

"Are you certain?"

"Of course. I asked him. He told me you hadn't done it. Naturally, I had to know before going on with the rest."

"The rest?"

"The firm. Father's work. Perhaps you haven't thought of it, but I am your boss now. And I don't happen to know what you and he were doing."

He hesitated before answering.

"I have a card." She reached into a pocket of her gown and showed him a red badge.

"How did you ever get that?"

"Father," she said. "At one time he and I were very close but I'm afraid—the last few months—we drew apart. That's why I need to know what you were doing."

"Androids," he answered, lowering his voice to a whisper, although they were quite alone.

"I know that much."

"A new model. Capable of being—well—soldiers. Ground soldiers. In the thick of battle."

She laughed in appreciation. "How ingenious. An army that cannot be killed. How close were you to completion?"

"The contract was signed yesterday. We've produced several prototypes and had intended to begin mass production as soon as the check cleared."

Again, her hand went into her pocket. She waved a sheet of yellow paper at him. "Here it is."

"You got it?" he asked, astonished.

"You think I'm callous but—well, Father's work was all he had."

"He died for it."

"You think spies killed him?"

He shook his head, determined to avoid the easy lie. "I hope you're not determined to continue his work."

"But I am. Aren't you?"

He shook his head. "I've given it a lot of thought. Did you know—I don't suppose you did—that Ted was having second thoughts himself? Two nights ago we had an awful argument. I think what happened was that Ted finally realized the significance of our work. With these androids, war is no longer an unthinkable proposition. It tips the scales—the balance of power— our way. Ted saw this and it frightened him. He knew what it would mean and it disgusted him."

"But he signed the contract. I saw it."

"Yes, because I made him."

"You?"

"Yes." Alec pointed at a wooden bench set against the high dirt cliff. "Why don't we sit down?" They were halfway up the hill. Another cluster of tourists sped past them. "Your father wasn't a strong man," Alec said.

"No," she said. "But all of that is past. I'm going to take over the firm. And I want you to help me." Her grief had totally faded now. Instead, her thoughts were as analytical and calculating as any Cargill had had. But he could also tell that she was speaking the truth.

"I don't know," he said.

"It will make you rich."

"I know that."

"But I don't want to rush you. I'll give you a week. It will take that long for the government to intervene with the courts and see that the will is promptly settled."

He had seen no way of bringing this up before, and there was no way now either—but keeping the truth from her did not seem fair. "You may be risking your life," he said.

"But you told me—"

"I said they weren't spies. They weren't. But these people . . ." There was no way he could explain any more fully.

But Sylvia did not force him. She said, "I don't care. I'll tell you the truth, Alec. Yesterday—after the police called me—after I had come to the office and answered questions—I saw that contract sitting on Father's desk. I'll tell you the truth: nothing mattered to me after that. I want money, Alec. It's the oldest form of motivation there is. I've been poor. All my life. And this is my chance to escape. I won't pass it up. I know that means I'm selfish, but nothing else matters as much—androids, war, even my father's death. He gave me nothing while he was alive. It wasn't entirely his fault, perhaps, but he didn't. I think he owes me this chance."

"I've been poor too," he admitted.

"Then you can understand."

"I was raised in a government home. My mother died giving me birth—I never knew my father."

"I'm sorry," she said, with what seemed to be genuine feeling. And yet her thoughts were as calculating as ever.

For the first time, Alec shied away from her. He stood up, saying, "I'll let you know my decision—in a week." But he thought he knew it already. He wasn't any less greedy than she—and not nearly so honest about it. He didn't want money—he could always find that. What he wanted—hadn't Cargill hinted as much?—was power.

She handed him a slip of paper. "My address and number."

"I'll walk you to a cab."

"Thank you."

In mutual silence, he led her down the hill.

six

Whistling a rather discordant tune—he didn't know what—Alec Richmond closed the office door and stepped down the corridor. It was late and the walkway was not moving. After seeing Sylvia home, he had decided to come here to catch up on his work. Going home had no longer seemed important. Once here he found it difficult to pull himself away. He had already missed dinner and then some. But if Anna was worried, why hadn't she called?

He couldn't answer that question.

"Stand right where you are," said a voice from behind.

Alec froze, feeling in the pit of his back the hard pressure of something small and round. A disembodied hand moved around his chest, easily penetrating the folds of his jacket. With practiced fingers, the hand emerged, holding the same gun with which Alec had killed Ted Mencken. He had intended getting rid of the weapon. How stupid to be carrying it so openly.

Alec started to turn around.

"I wouldn't," said the voice. It was like a cold, confiding whisper.

"Who are you? Do you want money?" But Alec knew that was too much to expect. Robbery was a rare event in this modern world. The chances of any particular man being robbed had recently been calculated at one in twenty thousand. Alec did not think he was lucky enough to be that man.

In confirmation, the voice giggled with real delight. "I'm already richer than you'll ever be."

"Then—" Alec knew it had to be one of them—one of the others. "Are you going to kill me right here?" The man—if that was what he was—radiated nothing.

"What do you think?"

"Did you kill Ted?"

"Who?"

40

"Ted Mencken. In that room—back there—yesterday afternoon."

"I thought you did it." But the voice laughed.

"Please," Alec began, but he suddenly felt a powerful odor tickling at his nostrils. Tears filled his eyes. He couldn't breathe. He reached for his neck but before he could manage the maneuver his feet left the floor. He thought he was a cloud. It seemed silly. He was floating up—racing to embrace the moon.

Then he did laugh.

"Gas," he murmured aloud. But before he could finish the thought, he was falling straight down.

He awoke relaxed, refreshed, as if he had spent a full night in unbroken dreamless slumber. A hot sun burned down brightly from above. He had to keep his eyes closed against the glare. There wasn't any wind. He tried to move his head but couldn't. Something was holding him. His hands—his arms—his legs. . . .

It was then he realized the yellow light wasn't the sun. He was inside a room, tied in a chair.

"Turn that away," he said, speaking with difficulty. He cleared his throat and tried again: "I can't see."

"Of course," said a voice. And the light did move slightly.

Alec opened his eyes and looked down. He was perched upon the seat of a high chair, like those in which babies were sometimes fed. Far below he could see the faint pattern of a carpet. The light continued to dominate everything he could see. It turned his flesh—the carpet, the chair—turned everything yellow. Beyond the light, he could see nothing.

The voice spoke from the darkness on the other side of the light. "We have a few questions to ask you, Alec. You will not mind answering, we hope."

He suddenly realized that he was alive. They hadn't killed him—why? Questions? What could they possibly want to know? This voice wasn't the same as the one which had greeted him outside his office—when?—hours and hours ago. This voice was shrill, distorted, as if its owner were a man barely clinging to the edge

41

of sanity. The tone of the voice frightened Alec more than anything.

No. That wasn't true. There was something much worse. Realizing this, he had to bite his lip to keep from screaming out. The silence. Beyond the light. There were men out there—at least one, but undoubtedly more—he knew that. But their radiations. Although he strained and strained his superior senses, he could find nothing: not a thought, not a feeling.

The voice spoke, casual sounds suspended in an utter void: "It will be better if you answer us."

"Who are you?" Alec cried. "What do you want with me?" He tugged at the ropes that bound his wrists but they would not budge. "Tell me—please."

"What?" the voice cried. "Tell you? No, no, it is you who must answer." Alec heard a sharp sound, like a man springing suddenly to his feet, filled with—what?—anger, no doubt. But he couldn't know that for certain. That was the awful part. This was much worse than being struck suddenly deaf or blind.

"All right," Alec said. "I don't care. Kill me. Ask me questions. I—"

"We will begin with the woman," said the voice.

"Yes?"

"The one you saw the day of your capture."

"Yes, she—" A disembodied hand came hurtling out of the blackness and struck his face. Alec cried out, hearing someone giggle. Another voice laughed. Alec struggled to keep his tears from blinding his eyes. There was blood on his lips.

"The questions," said the original voice.

"Yes," Alec said.

"Then tell us who this woman is."

"Sylvia Mencken. The daughter of my employer, Ted Mencken. The man you—you killed."

"A human?"

"Sylvia? Yes. Of course."

"And what did you tell her?"

"Nothing in particular. We discussed the firm. It's hers now. She's my boss."

The voice was growing increasingly frantic; hysteria

was not far away. "But are you not aware that such intercourse is strictly forbidden? Your Inner Circle has decreed that—"

"I couldn't very well wait for a vote," Alec said. "She asked to see me right away."

"And you told her—everything?"

"No."

"You told her you were a Superior. The Inner Circle. Their program, plans. You told her everything, didn't you?"

"No. Why should I—?"

"Liar!" Again, the hand. Alec saw it coming this time and was able to throw his head aside. He took the blow on his cheek. The flesh stung.

Inside Alec a terrible suspicion was growing. These men didn't intend to kill him, after all. They were not even the others. They were—

"What did you tell the police?"

Alec decided to act on his suspicion. Wasn't it better to know? "Everything," he said.

"What?"

"I told you—everything." And in his mind he conjured up a vision of his confession. Cargill sat across from him. His own hands waved like windmills as he spoke. "About the Superiors. The Inner Circle. Everything."

"No! You—!"

He shut down the vision. "If I'm the traitor you seem to think I am, doesn't that make sense? How can I be a traitor and keep my mouth shut all at the same time? Yes, I told Cargill everything. And Sylvia too. I tell everyone everything. I tell them all about you, Astor." And, saying this, he sat up as straight as he could and glared into the darkness, radiating as much hate as he had strength to create.

He heard one of them shout out, but Astor's voice—no longer distorted—was amused: "You are much more intelligent than you once were, Alec."

"I'm getting older. Now turn that light aside. And untie me."

"So soon?"

"Unless you still think I can't be trusted."

"No. We never did. But, Alec, you should know better than to violate our decrees. We—"

"Turn me loose, Astor."

"Certainly, Alec." The harsh light went out. A faint glow—emanating from across the ceiling—came instead. The round, moon-like face of Samuel Astor was smiling at Alec. Another pair of hands attacked his ropes.

"When I get loose, I ought to kill you."

"But, Alec," said Astor. "Can't you understand? We had to know the limits of your deviation."

"What deviation?"

"That woman. She—"

"How ridiculous can you get?" He sprang out of the chair, free now, and almost fell over. Standing on wobbly knees, he struggled to regain his balance.

"This is standard procedure," Astor said, coming over and roping an arm past Alec's shoulders. He patted him on the back. "An investigation. A punishment for your transgression. But—I am pleased to add—an initiation rite as well. Welcome—" Astor suddenly stuck out his free hand "—to the Inner Circle."

"What?" Alec mechanically accepted the proffered hand, shaking weakly. Turning away from Astor, he gave the room a close inspection. It was small—furnished in austere plastic—dully painted: a hotel room, no doubt. There were other men here too. He recognized Arthur Ramsey, second-in-command within the Circle. Antonio Martinez. Ernest Feralli. Axel Jorgensen. Chinua Nodawbe. Timothy Ralston. Chin Kao Lun. And the others. Yes, all of them were present: the entire Inner Circle.

"Shortly before your arrival," Astor was announcing, "we cast our ballots. The selection—tentative upon your innocence of any major transgression—was quite unanimous. You are one of us now, Alec."

Replacing his arm around Alec's shoulders, Astor steered him toward a connecting door. One of the others—Martinez—a small, light-skinned South American—opened the door and ushered them through. This room, not much larger than the first, was dominated by a long table; a dozen chairs had been neatly placed around it. Astor escorted Alec to a chair, then assumed his own place at the head of the table. One by one, the others drifted in and, when everyone seemed comfortable, Astor opened the meeting.

If any stranger for any reason—deliberate or not—had managed to sneak close enough to overhear the conversation that now took place, he would have learned nothing. During the course of the meeting, no more than a dozen decipherable words would be spoken. If any Superior's thoughts became too complex to be communicated simply through feeling, then a grunt, a half-word, a few casual sounds would be sufficient to get his meaning across in most instances.

Without words, Astor began: "I want to say that Alec Richmond has consented to attend his first meeting today. As you may recall, he was elected to our council recently because of the superb work he has accomplished out in California. Before we begin the actual meeting, I think we ought to stand and welcome him properly to the Circle."

This proved to be a signal for a brief orgy of handshaking, backslapping, friendly pats, and spoken congratulations. Alec came to his feet, accepting the plaudits as thickly as they arrived. The ceremony took only a brief moment. Soon, everyone was seated once more. Alec dropped down and clasped his hands upon the tabletop.

Astor said, "You may think us callous, Alec, but we are aware of the recent death of your employer. He was a human, but he had helped us, and therefore we're sorry he died. Still, the incident in no way detracts from the essential nature of your work. We understand the project has in no way been harmed."

"No," Alec said, keeping the fact of his ambiguous statements to Sylvia closely concealed. After all, he had never really intended to quit. Had he?

"But—" Astor waggled an angry finger "—I must state that your failure to communicate with us follow-

45

ing the incident severely damaged your application. If it hadn't been for the importance of the project ... well, you might actually have been turned down. When we spoke to Anna, she of course explained everything. Understanding, we could forgive."

"Anna told you."

"She explained your—ah—your difficulty."

He meant reversion. It wasn't a word any Superior cared to state specifically. Alec had difficulty concealing his surprised reaction. Anna must have thought quickly. Reversion indeed. He hadn't notified the Circle of Ted's death for a variety of reasons: lack of time, lack of interest, the fact that they would be of no help. But Anna had certainly saved him there. But if they had known the facts all the time, then why the stupid kidnapping, the absurd interrogation? He felt himself growing angry again and fought to control the emotion. This was hardly the time for an outburst of any kind.

"Thank you," was all Alec could manage.

"You're welcome," said Astor, nodding his acceptance. Around the table, the others did the same, as though Alec's gratitude was to be shared equally.

Astor stood, facing the entire council now. "But the purpose of this meeting is not to receive expressions of gratitude. Rather it is to take a glance at and then discuss the present international situation. I am pleased to be able to report—after considerable examination of the various nations concerned—that the world is closer to war at this point in time than at any other point in time in the remembered past."

The pleasure this announcement brought to the majority of the assembled Superiors was openly expressed. Some smiled, waved their hand, laughed, giggled, murmured vague syllables of expressive joy. Alec sat silently and motionlessly, his thoughts under rigid control; they knew how he felt.

"Now if you'll all please lean back," Astor said, "if you'll close your eyes, relax, and watch, I'll give you a brief resume of the present situation."

Astor was the only Superior to have perfected this

particular talent. It was this ability—more than anything else—which had allowed him to assume his place
at the head of the Circle. Alec did as directed: leaning
back, eyes shut, relaxed. In a moment, as if he were
dreaming, a vision began to form in his mind. Bit by
bit, the vision solidified, becoming more certain in
color and texture. Soon, the picture was quite clear. He
could see a long paved street. A caption at the bottom
of the picture identified the scene as Vienna. Above, in
the sky, the fierce growling of burning rockets drowning out the common noises of the street, an airplane
slashed through the clouds. The people in the street
paused and glanced up, many smiling at this loud
manifestation of their collective power. A moment
later, Vienna was gone; Berlin materialized instead. A
huge army marched through wide streets, heels slap-
ping out a rhythmic message. Tanks drifted languidly
through the air, floating past the army, like fat ducks
arranged for flight. Missiles rolled past. More planes
painted the sky with noise. It was an awesome spectacle of determined might. After Berlin, similar scenes
followed in neat progression: Paris, Madrid, Rome,
Lisbon, Copenhagen. Then Astor's voice: "The civilized nations of Europe, in conjunction with their
American allies, continue to mobilize." A Russian
army streamed past. "Manpower, though limited, is
strategically deployed. The most sophisticated legal
modern weapons are produced and distributed. In each
nation across the continent, the single word *war* rests
lightly, familiarly, upon the lips of the people. The recent reduction in energy resources, the scarcity and
continued expense of the most basic food items—these
factors have combined to cause the average European
citizen—particularly those past the age of con-
scription—to take a more militant stance than before.
A recent, successful propaganda campaign—source unknown—(embarrassed but proud giggling greeted this
allusion)—emphasizing the continuing upward spiral
of primitive nation birthrates has had a powerful effect
upon the development of a mature, pragmatic attitude

toward final war. In fact, according to many leaders of finance and industry—whose thoughts are easily penetrated, I may say—war has reached the point of verging upon absolute necessity. Only the known strength of the other side stands in the way of immediate attack. Should war occur—and I mean at this moment—the armies of the primitive world would swarm across Europe like hordes of invading insects. In Japan and Australia, the situation is even more difficult."

"Then why do you insist war is near?" asked a skeptical voice. The Russian army continued to stream past, an endless mass of green and brown.

"Because of this," said Astor. The vision was transformed. The interior of a large plant—a factory. Machinery—piston and electric—pounded, whirred, shrieked. Churning motors sent bright sparks flickering through the air. Huge transparent plastic vats filled with thick colorful liquids sat here and there across the concrete floor. Alec nearly laughed: the vision was an adolescent fantasy. This was hardly the way it really was.

But the primary vision—and this made Alec wish to laugh more than anything—the central element in the design—was the assembly line. Here, hooded and goggled men labored to mold separate human appendages into a whole man: hands, legs, heads, internal organs rolled down the conveyer belt. Alec groaned. Didn't Astor know any better? Or was this fantasy in fact deliberate? The scene—bright colors, huge shadows, flying sparks—was staggering in its impact, awesomely effective, an image from some gothic melodrama. Even Alec was not wholly unmoved by the vision.

"What is this?" asked a voice, in hushed tones. "Heaven? Or hell?"

"Neither," Astor said, without amusement. "This is our salvation: an android factory."

The Circle was confused; Alec could clearly sense their puzzlement as the conveyor belt continued to turn through the bright factory. Was it possible they didn't know? Astor had never informed them?

Abruptly, the vision faded. Alec opened his eyes, matching the gaze of the Superior who faced him across the table.

"I thought androids were stupid house servants," this man said.

Astor giggled. "Alec," he said. "I think you ought to be the one to tell them."

"These androids, I believe, are soliders," Alec said.

"Go on."

"I designed the model. They are foot soldiers, infantrymen, riflemen. Nothing complicated or difficult. The vision Astor showed you was an exaggeration. Production has not yet begun. The contract was only signed yesterday—the day before—whenever it was. The day Mencken was murdered."

"So that's why the others killed him."

"We thought it was another of their jokes."

"Their warnings."

"We thought they were just playing around."

Alec could sense their suppressed anger. They were not happy with Astor for keeping them in the dark. But such a technique was just like him. Astor equated power with knowledge and preferred keeping both as much to himself as possible. Alec did not think his attitude was far from wrong.

"So," said Astor, ignoring the gathering dissension, more amused by it than displeased, "the equation turns out brutally simple. We, the Superiors, will emerge from our time of trial ultimately victorious. How? This is the ironic part. Through the means of a species not only inferior to our own but also inferior to the dominant race on this planet: I refer, of course, to the android army. Such an army can lose and lose and lose and never stop coming. In a year's time—wouldn't you agree with that estimate, Alec?"

"At the very most. More likely, six months."

"In a year or less the first android divisions should be trained and ready to take the field. Kept in ignorance, the primitive world will be unaware of the menace until it is too late. Then, when the moment is ripe, a spark will ignite the general conflict. Full-scale war will rage across the globe." His voice, rising toward a crescendo, was filled with an ecstasy close to hysteria. "Armies will meet upon the battlefield, converge, clash. Cities will be destroyed. Entire nations engulfed by flames. The fighting will go on, the advantage rocking back and forth, the masses of the primitive world set against the android mercenaries of the civilized. Who shall win?" He laughed aloud. "That is the joke. No one will win—no one can—except" (another laugh, louder than before) "except us. After a year of war— two years at the most—the human race will turn in horror and fear, issuing a tearful plea for salvation. Perhaps they will ask their gods. It will be we who will answer. You. Me. Our race. The Superiors."

"But this spark," said someone—it was Axel Jorgensen, "what if it doesn't come? What if they don't fight?"

"Oh, that," said Astor, indicating with a wave how inconsequential it was. "That is already settled. The fuse lies in wait, ready to be fired. Shut your eyes again, please, and I will show you."

With the others, Alec prepared himself to receive another vision. What came confused him at first. A jungle setting. Then, through the deep foliage, another factory, as lacking in reality as the other. Past a high barbed fence. Through thick concrete walls lined with lead. Men—flashes of yellow skin, narrow eyes— dressed in radiation-proof garments. A huge oblong object, like an egg. It was a bomb. Alec knew. An atomic bomb.

"This can't be real," Alec said. Atomic weapons had been banned decades ago, before the need for war had reasserted itself.

"It isn't," said Astor.

"Then—"

"Look."

In the vision, one man stepped forward. Slowly, carefully, dramatically, he removed his face mask.

There was an audible gasp of surprised recognition. Alec contributed too. The face belonged to Thomas Mikoshai: a Superior, Inner Circle member.

"You can't do this," Alec said, weakly.

"The spark," Astor said, refusing to conceal his triumph. "You wanted it—there it is." The vision vanished. "Once the existence of this barbaric weapon becomes known—the location, by the way, is a jungle in Borneo—war will become inevitable. Our only problem is timing. We do not dare reveal this secret until the android army is prepared to take the field. Then, and only then, we can—"

"No!" Alec cried. "The whole idea is inhuman."

"Of course it is." Astor laughed and looked deliberately around the table. "Aren't we?"

"Not in that way."

"But it's your project," said one of the others. Jorgensen again. "You're not going to argue against it?"

"Yes. I am. I didn't know about any of this—this bomb."

"What did you think?" Astor asked. "I intended to use your army as a labor-saving device?" He chuckled loudly—for too long a time. "You could have refused the assignment."

"But—" Astor knew why Alec had not refused. If he had, he would not be sitting here now. The android army had got him into the Inner Circle—but now he fully intended to argue against it. "You all know my feelings. I've expressed them to each of you before."

"I had hoped," Astor said, "that your promotion might have affected your past immaturity. If I am wrong, I'm sorry. But you are a member of the Circle now—so speak."

"I will. But I don't see that it will make any difference. I have only one question to ask. Is it necessary? Do we have to destroy them? Is this horrible war we're so casually discussing really necessary? Can't any of you see how much easier—how much better—it would be if we simply helped them? Not all human beings are—"

"That was four questions," Astor said.

Martinez said, "Help them? Do that, and we die like witches. We burn at the stake. They hate us—fear us. Only fools cannot learn the lessons that history teaches."

51

"This isn't history," Alec said. "It's been a long time since any witch was burned."

"But they have not changed," Martinez said. "The old fears have not left them. I walk down the street—any street, any city—and I feel it there. Fear, hate. Anything they cannot understand. And we, by definition, are creatures they can never understand."

Alec fell back to his last and strongest ammunition. Another question: "And what about when it is over? When we have won?"

Astor, understanding immediately, went rigid with tension: "What do you mean by that?"

But Alec did not intend to stop until he was finished. Facing Astor, he plunged on: "Have all of you forgotten the most basic fact of all: we are doomed. All of us, sooner or later, are going to die. And afterward? Will there be another generation—further genetic freaks like ourselves? I don't know. Maybe there will be. But, if so, we will not be the ones to produce it. And what if there isn't? What if we are the last? Are we going to destroy the whole human race with nothing to substitute in its place? That is not only inhuman, it is monstrous. It is genocide conducted for no reason beyond brief and transitory power. That is why I say no. That is why I say we should drop this project right now, reveal ourselves selectively to humanity, and help them. In doing that—"

"Don't." Astor sprang suddenly to his feet. "Don't talk about that—don't mention it!"

"It's the truth," Alec said.

"No! *No, no, no!*" Astor's face turned a deep and ugly red. He seemed to be choking. The others stood up too. Astor's eyes bulged, his lips trembled, his whole body shook. He seemed to be trying to speak but the words refused to come. Stunned, Alec remained in his seat, staring unbelievingly at this unhinged, incoherent creature which had materialized, half-standing, at the head of the table.

Then Astor began to scream. His hands waved over his head, fists banging together, fingers tangling. Two of the others crept behind him. He continued to wail.

52

Tears ran down his cheeks in wide streams, though he did not appear to be weeping. The two men leaped forward. They caught Astor by the arms. Two more went for his feet, dodging kicks. Astor was lifted up, laid on the table. The four men held him there, pinned. He continued to twist and turn, like a man in the grip of a fit—he continued to scream.

Alec turned away from the sight.

The man beside him—Timothy Ralston—an American Negro from Wyoming—said, "You should never have done that."

Alec let his anger out: "It was the truth. What else was I supposed to do? If you people can't—"

"It's his calculations," Ralston said, calmly. "You have to remember. He had everything figured out. It fit. Only one point eluded him. Our curse. When you brought it up, he reverted. The rest of us knew."

"You mean this has happened before?"

"Astor? Yes, of course. He is brilliant but—well—erratic. Someday, I'm afraid, he won't make it back. We'll lose him."

"And that's fine with me," Alec said. He had seen quite enough of the Inner Circle for one day. Upon the table, Astor was slowly calming down, though one foot continued to thrash and kick, like the instinctive motions of a dead chicken. "I'm going home."

"I'll go with you," Ralston said.

Alec went out into the corridor, refusing to look back. The hallway was plushly decorated, lighted in a soft golden hue. A hotel—yes—and an excellent one. He waited impatiently for the elevator. Ralston joined him inside. They rode down to the lobby together. Crossing that plushly carpeted room, Alec started laughing, then couldn't stop. It suddenly seemed so funny. For years he had wanted nothing from life more than a seat on the Inner Circle. And now—at long last—he had attained that cherished goal. And for what? To do what? His first meeting and he had already driven the chairman into reversion and been forced to flee himself in a fearful rage.

Outside, he paused in front of the moving walkway—it was more than packed—and glanced up at the sky. The air was thick and black—the time seemed around midday—and he couldn't see the sun.

He shook his head, blinked, then looked again. Massive skyscrapers, old and ruined, sprouted from every corner. Upon the walkway, the flocks of pedestrians, hurtling past, kept their eyes averted toward the pavement, as if fearful of catching a fateful glance of something they might not be able to forget. Suddenly, from behind, a massive woman in a heavy armored coat crashed into him. He nearly fell. The woman sped past and leaped gracefully upon the walkway. Someone screamed.

Alec spun around, filled with sudden recognition: this wasn't San Francisco—it couldn't be—this was New York City.

But how—?

"Surprised?" asked Ralston.

"Last night—" he had forgotten about the other Superior "—I know I was in San Francisco."

"No," said Ralston. They both spoke complete English to avoid attracting attention. "That was days and days ago." He led Alec away from the walkway, back into the great shadow cast by the hotel awning. "The gas they bungled—the dose was too strong."

"Days and days?" Alec murmured, vaguely.

"A week at least."

"But I have to get home." He reached for his purse. "I don't think I have—"

"Oh, I'll be glad to loan you the fare. But first— well, I did follow you out here for a reason. There's something I want to know."

"Whether I'm going to quit the project."

"Yes," Ralston said.

Alec shrugged. "I don't see what point it would serve. You—Astor—he'd only find someone else. My work is nearly done. The patent belongs to my employer—his daughter now. If I quit, you'd run me out of the Circle. That wouldn't serve any point either."

"Then you'll continue with your work?"

54

"Yes." Sighing, Alec shook his head. "You can tell that to Astor, if you want."

"No. This was for my own information. I am, you see, in charge of—well—call it our investigative wing."

"You spy."

"Investigate."

"Use your own word."

"And there is a connection between your present intentions and another matter that has recently come to my attention. I want to warn you." Leaning close, Ralston whispered into Alec's ear: "Don't trust Anna."

"What?" Alec drew back as if stung.

Ralston pulled him back down. "She has been associating with this detective—this Cargill. I know it for a fact but I haven't told the others yet. This investigation is something I'm conducting on my own. Astor doesn't know about it."

"What?" Alec asked.

Ralston shook his head but answered: "The others. I'm trying to find out who they are. And I'm close, Alec, very close. A few more weeks and I'll have them."

"You think Anna's involved? That's incredible. I don't—"

"Not Anna. Cargill. He's mixed up in this somehow."

"How?"

"I don't know. Yet. But I will. I just wanted to warn you."

"But Cargill's investigating me. That's why he saw Anna."

"Three weeks ago? That's when he visited your house—the first time."

"And you don't know why."

Ralston shook his head. "I don't but—" he radiated confidence, "—I will." He stepped back suddenly. "But I better go now. Here." He pressed Alec's hand. "This will buy you a ticket home." He turned away, waving one brown fist. "Astor may want me."

"But, Ralston, I—" Alec started to pursue.

Ralston was too quick. He darted toward the hotel. He called back: "Don't tell her!"

Alec stopped, watching the other man disappear, swallowed up by the great bulk of the hotel. Then he hurried over to the walkway and leaped on board, refusing to concern himself with whom he might hit in the process. He landed safely, then let the walkway carry him. He didn't know if he was heading in the direction of the terminal and didn't care. He surrendered himself to this electronic destiny; it could carry him wherever it wished.

He had gone only a few blocks when the crowd, in mass, suddenly turned and looked straight up at the sky. Alec, in perfect conformity, looked too. A series of block letters was forming up there, bright red against the dank gray sky. He waited, reading along with the others, until the message was completed. It wasn't a news headline. It read:

AH TRAN IS COMING HERE
SOON

Beneath, appearing suddenly, was a huge banner: a photograph of Ah Tran himself. Alec peered deeply into the ageless features of this man who claimed to have a plan for the salvation of the human race, but the sky was too dark, the eyes too far away, the buzz of the crowd too distracting.

He could see nothing up there he had not seen before.

Then the walkway was moving too quickly and the message disappeared behind. Alec tucked his head into his shoulders and drifted lazily, effortlessly away.

seven

Passing easily through the glass wall, Anna Richmond entered the central garden and was immediately met by a cold wind that cut like ice through the thin fabric of

56

her gown. Holding her arms around her chest, she hurried to another place in the wall, where a dozen plastic dials were embedded in the soft wood. She turned one slightly to the left and the wind grew noticeably warmer. She touched another dial, letting her hand rest briefly, and was answered by the piercing shrieks of a flock of exotic birds. Then, the scene now properly set, she moved off into the high foliage. She stepped lightly, barely conscious of her own movements, lost in a trance. The effects of the sleeping drug Eathen had administered the night before had not wholly worn off. In particular, her toes were numb and tingly, as if asleep, and she shook her fingers constantly as she moved even deeper into the jungle of the garden. She could walk out here without thinking in any event. She found the carefully hidden paths and followed them with knowledgeable ease. They were as familiar to her as the pattern of veins on the backs of both hands.

She came to a place just beyond the creek where an anthill lay beneath a high willow tree. This was not her destination but, since she was here, she paused briefly and looked down at the hill. It was noticeably larger than the last time she had seen it, higher than her knees and as much as two feet across. The surface of the hill shifted constantly, the motion of the ants appearing systematic, certain, definite. She could have watched them for hours, but there simply wasn't time. What were they doing? Why were they moving? What was wrong with just sitting in the sun and enjoying the day? She laughed at herself—children asked questions like those. Adults were supposed to know the answers. What was wrong with her?

She found another trail beyond the anthill and followed that through a narrow gate in a tall hedge. This was the place she had wanted all along—a brief expanse of cool, shaded grass. She threw herself down, opened her mouth, and made a noisy yawn.

Directly in front of her, a round pale face materialized between the trunks of two trees.

"Oh, there you are," she said, waving. "I didn't know if you might've gone out."

"No," Eathen said, emerging wholly from between the trees. He came up to her, gait stiff and careful, arms held rigidly at his sides, and stood without moving. "I was waiting for you to wake up."

"And here I am." She slapped the grass. "Sit down." He did—stiffly.

"How late is it?" she asked. "I feel like I slept for hours and hours."

"It's four minutes after noon."

"Not so long—but I think the dose you gave me last night was too strong. I can't remember dreaming."

"You were very nervous."

"I was?" She shook her head. "Oh—oh, yes—now I remember. Alec. I was waiting for him. Is he home now?"

"No."

"He went out again already?"

"He never came home."

"Oh—oh, no." She broke off, gazing across the expanse to a tree, where a small silent bird hopped from frail branch to branch. "Poor Alec," she said. "Do you suppose I should phone the police? Maybe Inspector Cargill arrested him. Wouldn't that be funny? We'd have to stand bail."

"If he had been arrested, I am sure you would have been notified."

"True." She broke away from the hopping bird and slapped Eathen on the knee. "Besides, Alec didn't do it. The others did. Alec couldn't kill—not even a little bird."

"Inspector Cargill should not be aware of the others' existence."

"He shouldn't be—no. But he is." She nodded sharply to herself. "I'm sure he knows." She stood up, gesturing at Eathen. "But do come along."

Eathen went with her a brief distance through the woods to the place where, the night before last, she and Alec had viewed the procession of Ah Tran through the streets of Tokyo. She recalled how angry Alec had been at the trick she had played, splicing a sculptured tape of her own into the report of the real

58

event. She had thought it a very funny gag, even though the tape she had fashioned for herself to view hadn't worked out properly.

She sat down on one bench and told Eathen, "You sit over there." Even though the sun above was no more real than the moon at night, the atmosphere was totally different now—as different, she thought, as day and night. After dark, there was a feeling about this place—an aura of possible fantasy—as though reality were some wraith-like spirit of the day easily discarded once nighttime fell. There was nothing like that here now: the spirit of reality floated above, refusing to be dislodged.

"We're going to have another lesson," she told Eathen.

"Now?" he asked.

"It's why I brought you here. If you want to be human, you have to learn."

"All right," he said. "Whatever you wish."

She turned and faced the trunk of a fat tree directly behind and, with a flourish, struck the wood with a doubled fist. A small door popped open below where she had struck, revealing a set of dials embedded in a slab of steel. "Music?" she asked Eathen, past her shoulder, touching one dial lightly. "You seem to have the best response with that."

"Whatever you wish, Anna. But—" she almost sensed a radiated anxiousness "—will this take long?"

"I don't know." She was facing the tree, seeing if she could feel him again. "Why?"

"I thought I should inquire concerning Alec. He has never absented himself in this fashion before."

"Maybe he's found a friend." She was being deliberately callous. "Some fat, stupid, dense example of humanity. You know he claims to love them so much."

"That is possible," Eathen agreed.

"Forget about it," she said, angered that his brief radiation had been all. "Just sit back and be quiet." She turned the dial. "Here—listen."

She turned back to find Eathen sitting so stiffly on his bench that she had to remind herself that his backbone was no different from hers or anyone's—a formation of bone and nerve and cartilage. From the way he sat, it might have been a long iron bar or a lead pipe. Alec had told her often enough that—physically at least—androids were the same as humans. Grown not born—that was the only significant difference. It was in more abstract places that the two diverged: androids lacked humor and perception, the senses of irony and perspective, most emotions. An android could not laugh or cry or feel anger or joy or sorrow. But it wasn't only emotional. Looking at Eathen she could see that. It was physical too. Anyone meeting him for the first time would know at once what he was. Eathen would not need to speak or walk or even move—they would know. Nor did androids radiate. There were no feelings inside for a Superior to detect. That was what she wanted to change: she wanted to make Eathen into a human being.

The music was playing now. It wasn't a piece she knew—some old song—a guitar and singer. This was Alec's music—she preferred classical material herself. And not just in music either. Her preferences extended into painting and literature and film and architecture. In everything, really, except her own speciality. She couldn't prefer classical tape sculptures. There weren't any. The art form was barely a decade old.

She became aware of an assortment of visual effects playing across the air—an accompaniment to the music, no doubt. She looked at Eathen. His eyes were open but he seemed wholly unmoved by the music and the effects. She thought he was probably composing his thoughts, carefully studying and analyzing what he was feeling and hearing and seeing so that he could describe his reactions to her later.

She sighed. How ugly and familiar that was. Once upon a time, she and Alec had sat just like that, except then she was the one who had been analytical. He would play a particular song and, when it was done, demand to know her reaction. She had never shared his peculiar tastes; her criticism, she recalled, had been blunt and excessively personal. She had equated his preference for bad music (what she thought was bad music) with some monstrous flaw in his personality. Alec, in turn, had despaired of ever converting her from a frame of unreal snobbery into a taste for real, natural music.

It was their differing backgrounds that were to blame. Poor Alec, raised in a government home, one of those chilling replicas of army existence—complete with uniforms, pomp, promotions, ceremony, courts-martial, demerits. Quite a place. The children assigned to the home—there were several dozen throughout the nation—were most often the offspring of quota violators. Alec had been a little different from the others, though not much, and Anna had willingly listened—at least in those first years—to his embellished recollections of a real mother and father. The truth was, of course, that Alec, like almost all Superiors, had lost both his mother and father too early to remember them at all. Anna's own mother had died giving childbirth, while her father was reported to have fled soon after, leaving his only daughter (this was Anna) in care of two old acquaintances, the Millers, Kelly and Alice, a wealthy but not exciting pair who, whenever Anna brought up the subject of her parentage, changed the subject quicker than a bolt of lightning. Still, the Millers had provided Anna with an education and given her time in which to allow her artistic abilities to grow and mature. She owed them a lot, really. When she was growing up and displaying every indication of being as mad as a hatter—hearing voices where none existed, that sort of thing, answering questions before any were asked—and alternating fits of high mania and low depression—well, the Millers had always managed to forgive and forget or, at least, to ignore. Her toys had always been the best. They had given her—she was twelve or thirteen—a horse, with real hair and fluid gray eyes, that could be ridden. Later, when she began to sculpture tape, her tools had always been the very best. A good life. Compared to Alec's, a great one.

Which raised an intriguing question: if she hadn't

accidentally stumbled across Alec Richmond's path that one fateful day, what would her life have been? The chance of anyone discovering her without Alec's help was awfully small. No—she would have lived alone. Then what? Suicide? She had often contemplated the deed. Internment in an asylum? She had feared that since hearing the first voices as a young child. A grim life in any event—a horrible and tragic one.

But she had found Alec—or he had found her. The fateful moment had struck during her first and only semester at Berkeley. During those months of initial separation from the familiar faces of the Millers, she had become more and more convinced of her own inescapable madness. She recalled seeing a tape about—who?—some old lady novelist—a woman who had gone through life creating fine art and being as crazy as could be—both conditions occurring simultaneously. Obviously, Anna had been deeply impressed. *Me, too,* she had thought, conceiving of herself following the footsteps of this now dimly recollected woman into the obliterating waves of the sea. But great art would have to come first, so she had spent most of her days at Berkeley ignoring her assigned studies and concentrating instead on producing her first major tape sculpture.

All of this had occurred prior to that fateful day. She had been walking down a certain street, headed for some forgotten rendezvous—no, she remembered now—it was a tennis match with a roommate—feeling no less crazy than ever—forced to suffer the passing whims of every stranger—unable then to resist at all—a bomb of dull grayness as some humble man slouched past—then a flash of someone young and bright and cheery—then a smash of green prurience—nearly naked in white bikini shorts and halter for the tennis match—and, finally, unexpectedly, tremendously, Alec.

Who had stopped. At the same instant, as they passed, both had immediately known the truth, glimpsed a matching soul, felt the presence of the other.

It was hard at first to speak, but finally it had all come out—no need for words even then—and they had gone off to a small cafe to chatter incessantly the remainder of the day. Alec had told all; she did too. He revealed the existence of the Inner Circle of Superiors. "You're not crazy, Anna," he had said. "If you are, so am I, and dozens more. We're the only sane ones. That's the point. It's the rest—the poor humans—who are crazy."

So she was cured. Just like that. In a matter of minutes. The world's greatest psychiatrists would have gone mad with envy had they known of Alec's ability. Three weeks later, in deep gratitude, she had married him.

When Alec was still a small child in the home, the Superiors had found him and told him what he was. That was the significant point—wealth meant nothing, really—where their backgrounds hopelessly diverged. Anna had lived eighteen years in madness and despair; in comparison, Alec had lived those same years possessed of the positive certainty of his own innate superiority. Because of that, nowadays, he could afford to condescend. He could say humans were good at heart and ought to be helped.

Arthur Ramsey, a frail old Inner Circle member, was National Home Director. He was the one who had discovered Alec. But Ramsey and the others had never had the slightest inkling of her existence. She should have been in that same home that housed Alec, but her father, for unknown reasons, had chosen to permit her to grow up in an atmosphere of wealth and promise. Had he known what that meant? Had he known what such a life would do to her?

Within three months of the wedding day, Anna had realized that the only reason she and Alec were together was because he had chanced to pass her that day. If it had been Arthur Ramsey instead, she would probably be married to him now. She did not love Alec. Neither did she hate him. She felt—as far as he was concerned—quite empty inside. And since, at least back then, neither was able to conceal a strong emotion from the other, Alec had soon learned how she felt. That had put an end to their marriage and now, years later, Alec was missing and she didn't know where or why, or care.

The music suddenly ended in a burst of color. Anna sighed and looked up and saw, with a start, that Eathen had disappeared. The bench he had occupied was now quite empty.

"Eathen!" she called. "What happened to you? Where—?"

He suddenly appeared across from her, passing between two tree trunks.

"Where have you been?" she said, angrily.

"I thought I heard the chimes sound."

"I didn't hear a thing."

"But someone was there."

"Who? Alec?"

"No, Inspector Cargill."

"Is it about Alec?" She stood up hastily and peered into the woods behind Eathen, as if searching for something lost.

"I wouldn't know," he said.

"Then bring him out and I'll ask him." She sat down.

"Bring him out here?"

"Yes. Of course. Why not? Do as I say. This isn't our private frolicking place."

But Eathen had already gone to fetch the visitor.

eight

Cargill first materialized as a vague shape flickering between the trees. He approached alone; a tiny white point—his head—swam through a sea of green. But, at last, a final tree slid from his path and he emerged, fully revealed, dressed in his official black burlap, a silver badge pinned demurely to his chest.

Anna said nothing. She allowed Cargill to come forward, entering the clearing on fastidious tiptoes, as though this were a sacred place and he were violating some shameful privacy. He bowed, nodded, smiled. His eyes darted suspiciously, peering into the dark shadowed places of the garden, but these anxieties—if they were real—failed to be reflected in the feelings he radiated. The control he exercised over his mind—as always—astonished Anna. Unlike Eathen, Cargill clearly possessed such things as thoughts and feelings. Yes, she could sense them vaguely, lurking down below. But the content of his inner life—its significance—that was firmly hidden from her view.

He had nearly reached the empty bench, mouthing her name as he came, when she stood up, towering high above him, gazing down at the pink smooth dome of his skull. "Well," she said, "where is he?"

Cargill feigned surprise. (His radiations remained unchanged.) "Your father?" He glanced furtively up, avoiding her eyes.

She shook her head and pointed to the empty bench. As he moved off in the indicated direction, she spoke to his back: "I mean Alec."

Cargill seated himself with deliberation, smiling a grin of achievement when he seemed securely lodged: "Who?"

"My husband. Alec. He went to see you yesterday and hasn't been home since."

"Sylvia Mencken," Cargill mumbled. He did radiate something: surprise.

"Who?"

"Mencken's daughter." He adopted a stiff, official tone. "I requested her presence yesterday in order to identify the body. I arranged that her appointment should coincide with Alec's, a saving of both time and money. Both accompanied me to the morgue. When they left, they went together."

"Is that where he is now?" she asked, her voice dropping to the level of a harsh whisper. It seemed so ugly—so base. How low would Alec choose to stoop?

"I haven't the slightest idea," Cargill said. "They left the morgue together. But they may have separated before they reached the bottom step of the Hall."

"But you don't believe that."

"I told you that I didn't know." He was plainly impatient and willingly radiated the fact. "Your husband—his present or past whereabouts—is not my concern. I was not hired to search for him or to prevent him from getting lost."

Eathen had joined them, standing unobtrusively at the edge of the clearing, so quiet and motionless that Anna would never have noticed him if her eyes had not happened, by chance, to stray past that point. But Cargill knew he was there. He didn't look. She sensed his sharp awareness. He knew.

Sighing, she attempted to impart the impression of dismissing the previous subject. "Then what did you come here to say?"

"This." Reaching into the billowing folds of his burlap garment, he removed a folded slip of paper. "A clue."

"Well—what is it?" Deliberately impatient.

"The name of your father." Without modesty.

"His name?" Now she really did manage to dismiss Alec from her thoughts. "I can't believe it. How——?"

"I have my methods," he said, proudly.

"Then he's actually alive?"

Cargill shook his head. "I'm afraid I can't say."

"Well, what can you say?"

"I told you—his name. Beyond that—to carry the investigation further—it will be a complex and time consuming process. I—"

"You want more money?"

She nearly laughed at the anger he radiated. *Touché!*

"If it becomes necessary, I will inform you without hesitation," he said.

"I'm sorry. Please continue."

"Thus far, I have traced the name through our national network with, of course, negative results. I have contacted most of the networks in the civilized nations with similar results. I have not tried the primitive nations, but I will. Their recordkeeping is notoriously— well—primitive, but I suspect we will pick up the scent over there. My time, however, is severely limited. When I accepted this assignment, I believe I informed you that any private work I choose to undertake must assume a subsidiary priority in relation to my official duties."

"Yes, yes. But—when? That's what I want to know."

"Oh, soon." He dismissed any strict construction of timekeeping with a wave of the hand. "I must complete this Mencken investigation first."

"But that may not be for months."

"Oh, no, sooner, much sooner than that."

"You mean you know who did it?"

"Oh, yes."

"Who? Alec?"

He shook his head.

"I asked who."

"If I were free to tell you that, I wouldn't be here. I would be making an arrest." He opened the slip of paper he had held in his hand throughout and read to himself.

"The name," she said, impatient once more.

He held the paper out to her and said, "Walsh. James Henry Walsh."

She laughed, taking the paper but not bothering to read. "That means I'm Anna Walsh."

"No, Richmond," he corrected. Then he went on: "I can further provide you with a detailed sketch of the man's life up until he was twenty-three. That would be four years prior to your birth."

"Did he attend a government home?"

"What makes you think that?"

"Nothing—a theory."

"He did not," Cargill said. "His parents died when he was young, but an aunt and uncle raised him."

"What if he's dead?"

Cargill shrugged. "Dead, alive, it makes no great difference to me. I'll find the body—presuming there is one—and ensure that it's his. In any event, I will follow the case to its very end. I always do."

"I'm glad to hear that. But—well—this whole thing

has become rather difficult. Since you started investigating Alec too. If he knew you were here, he'd be very upset. Enraged."

"Perhaps he does know." Cargill met her gaze. "There's a man watching your house, you know."

"No," she said. "I didn't know."

"A small man. A Negro. Very short hair."

"Timothy Ralston," she said, without meaning to speak aloud.

"Ah, I thought I knew him."

"You know Ralston?"

He waved his dismissing hand again. "Only slightly but—if it is your wish—I can promise not to reveal our relationship to your husband in any way."

"Yes. Yes—I would appreciate that." But if Ralston knew, that meant the Inner Circle knew. Would they tell Alec? If—that is—they could find him.

"And?" Cargill nodded toward Eathen.

"I trust him totally," Anna said. "Eathen and I have no secrets."

"Very good." Cargill stood, brushing at his clothes. "I will send you the report to which I referred within a few hours. Whenever I have further information to impart, I will call."

"Fine." Anna stood too. "Eathen—see that Inspector Cargill reaches the terminal safely."

"Oh, I can handle myself," Cargill said. He turned and hurried back toward the house, almost sprinting.

Anna whispered: "Go with him. Make sure he gets on a hovercraft. Don't leave till he does."

"Yes," Eathen said, rushing after Cargill. From where she sat, Anna could hear the inspector's stubborn protests. But Eathen would surely win out in the end. He was quite incapable of disobeying any request she made of him.

A moment later, experiencing the totality of silence around her, she realized that she was alone—really alone—for the first time in months. The house and garden were hers.

What was it? Her father? Just a silly obsession? Or was it really important—would it help her?

Her interest had been aroused some months ago. Mrs. Miller had died and, while exploring some old papers, Anna had chanced upon a brief typewritten note, unsigned and undated. The first few paragraphs had briefly described the pleasant state of the weather in some unnamed locale. It was the final paragraph alone, she knew it by heart, that had spoken directly to her: "I trust my daughter is well and giving you no more trouble than might ordinarily be expected. It remains my fond hope that it will someday be possible for me to see Anna but until then I am convinced she will continue to receive excellent care from you."

She had immediately searched the remainder of Mrs. Miller's effects but that one letter had been the only one. For weeks afterward, she had carried the single crumpled page with her everywhere. From various acquaintances, she had learned of Inspector Cargill. Contacting him, she explained the situation and he agreed to accept the case. She had really expected nothing. But now he had come and, without prelude, given her a name. James Henry Walsh. She uttered the words aloud.

She had told Alec nothing. Why? For many, many reasons: because she seldom told Alec anything; because he would no doubt interpret her obsession as evidence of reversion; because Alec, like herself, had been abandoned at birth, and yet he had never made the least effort at uncovering the secrets of his past. No, if she told Alec, he would tell the Inner Circle and that would be the end of it. They did not like to have their theories challenged, especially those that were most obviously weak. Maybe Alec believed what they told him: that Superiors are always abandoned children because their parents, sensing the strangeness of their offspring, grow fearful and choose to desert. That was what the Inner Circle said. She didn't think it made the least amount of sense, that it was simply a dumb subterfuge to avoid admitting ignorance. Why should the parents manage to detect so rapidly what hundreds of others—home officers, in particular—never noticed? And why was it invariably true? Every known Superior—

more than three hundred—had been discovered without known or visible parents. The national average for abandoned children—she had checked—was barely thirty percent. It didn't make sense. And she intended to find out why. She intended to find her father and ask him.

It was time to go inside. The wind seemed chilly once again. She was starting to shiver. Standing, she took the most direct path to the house and stepped quickly inside.

In the living room, she found Eathen. He was holding a heavy sheet of pink paper in his hands, staring down at it as though confused.

"What is that?" she said.

He looked up in surprise, plainly not having noticed her before. He shook his head desperately. Could he be afraid?

"Give it here," she demanded.

He hesitated, then passed her the sheet.

She read:

THE MESSIAH IS COMING!
THE WORLD MUST LISTEN TO THIS MESSAGE! AH TRAN!

The handlettering was crude, childish scrawls. Beneath the words was a photograph, a black-and-gray portrait of an ambiguously smiling face. The eyes were like the endless tunnels one sometimes followed in dreams. Who was this man? What was he? Messiah? Or devil?

Shaken, she crumpled the sheet and let it fall at her feet. "Where did you get this?"

"Inspector Cargill gave it to me."

"To you? Whatever for?"

"He told me—told me I should find out more about this man. That he could help me."

"How?"

"He didn't say."

She looked at Eathen carefully, trying to decide

70

whether he was lying. But, of course, there was really no way of knowing. And why should he lie?

The phone rang. Anna waved at Eathen, indicating he should answer it. She remained in the living room, lost in thought, until he returned.

"Yes?" she said. "Who is it?"

"Samuel Astor, Anna. He wishes to speak to you right away."

"Tell him I'm not here. Tell him I've thrown myself into the ocean."

"He says it's very urgent."

"Oh, no," she said, but went to answer the phone.

nine

Am I reverting? Anna Richmond wondered, as the elevator continued to ascend the outer wall of the building. *Is this what it is like?*

Eathen was standing beside the outer glass wall of the elevator, his gaze riveted by the unfolding panorama of the great city. He pointed at some famous object, spoke its name, but Anna shook her head; she didn't want to know anything. A terrible tenseness gripped her muscles. She knew she was shaking like a tall building in an earthquake. Maybe this building. Any building. There hadn't been an earthquake in the city for more than fifty years. One was supposed to be due anytime. *No,* she thought, nearly uttering the word aloud. *I can't do it. I don't want to.*

"Anna, is something wrong?" Eathen asked, turning away from the glass wall. She sensed his radiated concern—strong, more so than ever before. "Can I help?"

She shook her head. "I'm all right."

The long trip was the cause. She ought to have known better—really. It had been weeks and weeks since she was last out of the house, but still it wasn't until they'd boarded the hovercraft—crammed with the crush of morning commuters—that she'd realized how much worse it was now. The people who surrounded her were no longer separate identities to be recognized, probed, or ignored. Instead, each now had the appearance of some unavoidable mass of thought and feeling—a vast, bulky object—that seemed to crowd around her physically, pressing down with a heavy weight, forcing any thoughts of her own out of her mind. When they reached the city, it was worse, and Eathen had led her to the waiting cab as if she were blind or crippled. Here in the building it was better. There was only herself—which she could bear—and Eathen's faint radiations. Vaguely, she could sense others in the building as the elevator soared past floor after floor of tiny apartments. But they wouldn't let her stay in this cozy elevator forever. She recognized this. They were going to make her leave again.

"Are you sure—?" Eathen began.

"Yes." She cut him off sharply. "I told you I'm fine."

Now the elevator stopped. Anna wobbled dangerously as the doors parted. She peered out into a bright, wide corridor.

"This isn't right," she said, shaking her head.

"No." Eathen pointed at the indicator upon the elevator control panel. It registered 58. "I thought you told me apartment 5890."

"I didn't." Was there any point to lying now? She sighed. "All right—I did."

"Then this is it."

"Yes. Yes, I see." She drove herself forward—out of the elevator—into the corridor. Behind, the doors clanged shut with nasty finality. The elevator zipped away, speeding downward. The gaping hole in the wall through which they had entered closed like a healing wound.

Eathen pointed: "This way, I believe."

She stood her ground, refusing to budge. "I want you to stay here."

"Stay?"

"It's none of your business."

"But—" She sensed his concern.

72

Reaching out, she touched his arm warmly. "I'm sorry, Eathen, but this is an assignment." She tried to smile. "If Astor knew I'd let you come, he would take my head. You shouldn't know about any of this."

"But I—"

"Look, all I'm going to do is tell her what I'm supposed to tell her about Alec. They don't want her to worry. So it won't take more than a couple seconds."

"You should have just called her. There was no need to make you come down here."

"I wanted to come. It's better in something like this to stand face-to-face." Again, she touched his arm in a reassuring way. Oh, why was all this necessary now? Just last night—she had finally played for him some of her music—his feelings had finally been aroused. Was it necessary that they quit now? What was more important? Astor's silly plot, or the creation of a new race? "Look," she cried, spreading her arms over her head. "I'm not even armed. I won't hurt her."

"I never though you would," Eathen smiled. She had taught him that—smiling—but the gesture still seemed cold; there was no feeling on the other side of the lips.

"Of course not," she said.

With obvious hesitation, he stepped back and stood against the wall. "I'll wait here."

"Good. And—I won't be long."

"No."

"I'll be right back."

"Yes."

She meant every word she said but took only a few steps—turning a corner so that Eathen could not see—before she collapsed in a fit of silent giggling. She lunged against the soft, padded wall, restraining herself tightly, avoiding making any sound that would bring Eathen running. But what was so funny? Why was she laughing like this? She didn't know, and maybe that was what was funny. Then slowly, piece by piece, like the reconstructed parts of a jigsaw puzzle, she reformed herself, regained control. She straightened up.

She moved away from the wall and stood as stiff as a soldier. She marched off—down the corridor.

"I'm fine," she whispered to herself. "I'm not going to do anything wrong."

Apartment 5890 fitted neatly into a snug corner.

She knocked on the door.

A moment later: "Who is it?"

She answered boldly: "Anna Richmond."

The door opened instantly. The face that appeared confirmed all Anna's expectations: Sylvia Mencken was indeed a beautiful woman. And her radiations—Anna stepped back: there weren't any.

She wasn't—she couldn't be—she was a human being. So how—?

"Won't you come in," Sylvia said.

"Yes, yes," said Anna, hurrying past. The apartment was a blank, impersonal place—a pair of rooms, with the bed occupying a sunken place in the first. Anna moved around and found a chair against one wall. Across the room, hanging straight in the middle of her gaze, was some horrendous old painting: shallow-faced children with huge staring eyes confined by barbed wire.

"I find it amusing," Sylvia said. "And ugly. People back then—their minds were tepid."

"I guess so," Anna agreed, trying to shake the painting from her gaze.

"I hate the past," Sylvia said with feeling.

"Yes, but I came here to tell you—"

"You don't drink?" Sylvia, empty and silent, stood above her, looming like a grinning bird of prey.

"Yes, yes, I do." She eagerly clutched the proffered straw. "Please—anything."

Smiling, Sylvia disappeared into the second room. Glass clinked—ice rattled.

Is it me? Anna thought. She concentrated but—no—she could feel them: the others in the building. It was Sylvia—there was just nothing there.

"Here you are," Sylvia said, returning with a glass. Anna drank tentatively, failing to recognize the liquor. It was sweet.

74

"Alec is in New York," she managed.

"Yes—yes, I know."

"He wanted to call you but wasn't able to get through."

"Of course."

Anna recited her lines the way Astor had stated them: "An overload on the New York to San Francisco circuit. But he was able to reach me on a private line."

"I see, but—"

"He didn't want you to worry. He's sorry about missing work, especially at this time. But he'll be back. Soon. Very soon."

"When?" Sylvia asked, bluntly. Anna wished she would sit down, do anything, not just stand looming there.

"I'm sorry—I don't know."

"Why is he in New York?"

"I don't know that either."

Sylvia smiled and for the first time Anna caught a firm radiation. It was strong too—there was no way of missing it: pity.

"But he'll be back," Anna said, desperately trying to retain control of the situation.

Sylvia nodded and backed suddenly away, coming to rest underneath the painting of the hollow-eyed children. "Why don't you tell me something about Alec? We'll be working together now—I ought to get to know him."

"What do you want to know?" Anna asked, helplessly. Sylvia was radiating clearly now, but each emotion came so strongly that Anna had no chance to identify it before another had taken its place. It was like standing on the beach in the middle of a storm. Wave after wave of feeling came crashing relentlessly down upon her.

"Oh, anything. The kind of food he likes. His favorite color. Or, astrology? Do you believe in that?"

"No," Anna said, trying to watch her words carefully. It seemed—no matter what she said—that it was wrong. "I don't see any sense to it."

"But that's just the point," said Sylvia. She wore a long, tight, black gown that bared her arms and neck while keeping her legs concealed down past the ankles. As she spoke, she moved back and forth underneath the painting, shifting sidewise, not pacing, almost dancing, a graceful mocking motion. "I believe in anything that doesn't make sense. Astrology. Magic. Numerology. Any form of fortune-telling. Even the bumps on a man's head. Or Ah Tran and his cyclic theories. Do you know him?"

"Yes. I mean, no."

"That's why I appreciate paintings such as—" she gestured at the wall above "—that one. People tell me that art is a way of bringing meaning into life. I don't see that. I want my art to drive it away. That's why I cannot appreciate your sculptures—and I've seen every one you've done. They make too much—way too much—sense for me."

"I'm sorry," Anna said.

"Then do tell me about Alec."

"I—I wouldn't know where to begin." The truth was that Anna couldn't remember Alec. Underneath the awful assault of this woman's radiations, she could remember nothing.

Sylvia smiled and moved away from the wall at last. Once more she was standing in front of Anna. "I want to do you a favor."

"What?"

"Oh, nothing." She went to a small table in the center of the room and scribbled a note, which she brought to Anna. "Here you go."

Anna did not look. "What—what is it?"

"Where to find your father."

"My father? You know about—?"

Sylvia held up a hand. It was the same as a command. Anna fell silent.

"And now that you know," Sylvia said, "you can tell Inspector Cargill that you will need his services no longer. He is an evil man, Anna. You should best beware of him. You will tell him to drop the search."

"Yes." There was no other choice.

Sylvia laughed. "Not that he would ever have found him anyway."

Anna said, "Yes." It was the only word she knew. She was suffering from an awful headache. It felt as if someone's fingers had penetrated her skull, that they were moving across her mind, smoothing the wrinkles, crushing her feelings. "Yes," she said, with sudden conviction. "You are right. Yes, I understand. Yes, yes, yes."

When Anna met Eathen beside the elevator, she did not give him a chance to ask questions. She told him straightout: "It was easy."

"You told her?"

"Oh, yes."

"And she didn't ask any questions? Why he hadn't called her? What he was doing in New York?"

"She accepted everything I told her." She laughed, signaling for the elevator to come and take them down. "She's just a woman."

"What's that?" Eathen asked, suddenly. He was pointing at her hand.

"Oh, that." Anna raised the note and read the now familiar name and address written there. It was important—wasn't it?—she tried to remember. "Oh, that's my father."

"Your father?" The elevator arrived. They stepped inside. Eathen grabbed her arm. "That woman knew your father?"

"No," said Anna. Eathen's radiations were too strong. She wished he would go away and let her think in peace. "It was Inspector Cargill. He knew."

"Cargill was there?"

"Yes."

"But what—?"

"He was there." She could see him clearly, dark burlap, silver badge, standing, writing the note. "I saw him. He was investigating the murder. Why shouldn't he be there?"

Going down, the elevator was much faster. They stepped immediately onto the street. Eathen glanced behind.

77

"That man is still there," he said.

"Ralston? He saw us?"

"He must have."

"Oh," she said. "Oh, no." But it didn't really seem very important. No—not really.

ten

Before making himself venture out into the garden to look for them, Alec was determined to search every room in the house first. There were thirty, including rooms especially created for dining, bathing, sleeping, eating, studying, meditating, and tumbling. One room, on the far side of the house, was a vast ballroom, specifically designed for formal dancing. He and Anna had never made use of the room. It was the last place he inspected, but neither Anna nor Eathen was here either. He paused in the center of the vast, high-ceilinged room and looked at the outer wall. They had to be out in the garden.

That was the last place in the world he felt like going now, but after so long an absence, he could hardly come home and not inform his wife. Or could he? Why not? Did she even care?

While making up his mind, he roamed through the dusty room and uncovered a long forgotten bottle of Scotch tucked away in one dark corner. He popped the cork and sniffed the stem. It smelled good. He sat on the slick, polished floor and took a tentative swallow. He smiled. It was good. Another swallow. Still good. Another.

Finally, having formed a decision, he pushed the bottle aside and stood up. He retraced his steps to the place where the transparent wall afforded immediate access to the garden. He stepped unhesitantly forward, letting the feeling of warmth that flowed, tingling, through his blood drive him ahead. Cupping his mouth with his hands, he called:

"Anna!"

78

A squadron of flying ants—he thought that's what they were—buzzed around the top of his head. He swatted one, then ducked past the rest, hurrying down a wide pathway, which gradually narrowed as he continued. He kept his senses carefully attuned, expecting at any moment to be confronted by Anna. She had to be out here; she couldn't very well be trying to hide. He called her name again. Immediately, he felt the radiated presence of someone else—a dim and distant mind—a stranger. Who? He stopped and tried to penetrate farther, but the radiations were dim and uncertain. He shook his head and continued forward, following a sharp turn in the path.

He nearly ran right into Anna.

She was seated in front of a high, blinking, pulsating machine, which Alec recognized as a device used for editing separate tape sequences into a draft sculpture. It was good to see Anna working again. Her eyes were fastened to the protruding lens of a scope. She peered down deeply into the dark innards of the machine. Eathen sat on the grass at her feet.

With a start, Alec realized that the strange presence—the unknown person whose radiations he had earlier felt—was Anna.

What had they done to her?

He stepped forward, genuinely concerned, when she turned suddenly in her seat and glared at him.

"Now where have you been?" she said, coldly.

"I—" He stopped, unable to continue. He took a deep breath, fighting the dulling effects of the whisky. "I went to the office first."

"Wouldn't your war wait?"

"Astor ordered me to."

"Was she there?"

"Sylvia. Yes—of course. I called her ahead of time. Is there anything wrong with that?"

"You called her—but not me?" Before he could reply, she waved a hand, dismissing the question. She said, "I assume, then, that she told you."

"Yes," he said.

"Everything?"

"I suppose so."

Anna shrugged and turned back to the machine. Eathen, at her feet, was smiling up at Alec, but the gesture—on his lips—was a cold, dead thing.

"Stop doing that," Alec told him.

Around the three of them, a high circle of trees rose in a single, sheer mass, like the walls of a deep canyon. Directly overhead, the moon sat big and golden in the sky. From the silver haze that circled the disk, he gathered that this must be the real moon tonight. Anna had taken the risk of lowering the dome. The stars, as well, seemed peculiarly bright and far away.

"Anna," he said, when he saw her lean back in the chair. "Why did you—?"

She spun around, her defenses momentarily slipping. Alec was appalled by the ugly, chaotic, senseless mass he saw inside her mind. What had happened to her? Could she be reverting all the way at last? Her aura genuinely frightened him; he kept his own feelings under stern control.

"Why did I tell her I was leaving you? Is that what you want to know?"

"Yes," he said softly.

"Because I am," she said. "By tomorrow evening, I will be gone."

"But—" he struggled to find the right words "— why?"

"Because you disgust me. No—I shouldn't say that. I should say that it's your hypocrisy that disgusts me."

"What do you mean by that?" He tried to sound angry, but couldn't—couldn't even feel angry. When Sylvia had told him what Anna had said, he had been angry then. But not now. Not sitting across from her and seeing her as she was and, most importantly, feeling her. He let her speak freely.

"I can't tell you everything I mean," she said. "There isn't enough time for that. But your attitude on the war. You claim to be opposed and yet there isn't anyone working harder to bring it about."

"You know why—"

"No," she said, bluntly, meeting his gaze. "The fact is that I don't know."

They had never talked this way before—so openly and bitterly. Her contempt was so immense he could not fight it. One person can argue with another only when there is some form of mutual respect between them and, as a result, some possibility of winning the other over. Alec could see that this condition no longer existed with Anna.

"You tell me what I'm supposed to do."

"Refuse to make the androids."

He could tell that she was not only speaking honestly—truly—but that there was far more to it than that. He could almost sense the presence of some great barrier in her mind. She was speaking around this—unable to penetrate its mass—fighting a great battle with every word.

"Then Astor will just find someone who won't argue with him. I'm only one person."

"Yes, you are now—but you don't have to be. Talk to some of the others. Try to explain how you feel. Not all of them—us—are like Astor."

He laughed, unable to hide his own skepticism. "Aren't they? Are you so sure? They're Superiors—that's all any of them know—and they want power."

"Don't you?" she asked.

"I don't know."

"Can't you find out?"

He shook his head. "That's what I'm waiting to see."

She reached out. He came closer. She touched his hand. "Alec, I'm sorry it has to be this way. I wish it—none of it—had ever happened."

"What?" he asked.

She shook her head. Though her mouth opened, no words came out. Her feelings seemed muted now, as if the barrier whose presence he had sensed earlier had moved inward and smothered everything else. "Stay here," she said. "I want to work and I don't like doing it alone."

"What about him?" Alec pointed at Eathen, who had hardly moved in all that time.

"I want both of you to be here." She turned slowly back to the editing machine. Alec remained as he was, more than willing to honor her desire. The hate he had felt for her was wholly dissipated now. When Sylvia told him that Anna had visited her during his absence and said horrible, dreadful things about them both, he had come here prepared for a final showdown. But Anna had deflated him at once. He had intended to order her to leave; she had told him she was going. After that, was there anything more he could possibly say?

As she worked, Anna radiated an aura of inexplicable, unstated serenity, as though she had chosen to surrender herself up to some great inner urging. Maybe it was better this way—not only for her but for him too. Hadn't they both managed to get almost everything into the open through the surest means available—by talking? Wasn't it easier to relax now, with nothing bottled up inside?

But had he really told her everything? Or very much of anything? He had to admit—at least to himself—that he had not. Nor would he. Why? Perhaps because he was afraid that Anna would manage to penetrate his carefully erected defenses. She would glimpse the truth of his real feelings, and this was not something he cared for anyone to know.

Let the war come, he thought. Hadn't the human race—didn't the present state of the world testify to this—hadn't they proved themselves unworthy to rule? What sort of world was it, governed by a single species and yet divided into two warring factions? The one rich, the other poor. The civilized world and the primitive. Why did it have to be that way? He knew history—was aware of how it had developed—but history could not explain why the situation had to remain unchanged. And could a world divided against itself ever survive for long?

He didn't think so. He thought it would have to fall. Android soldiers or not. A-bombs or otherwise. As surely as the Earth turned, it was coming—the end was coming.

So didn't the choice really lie between chaos and order? The end was predetermined—but the postscript was as yet unwritten. Wasn't that the real mission of the Superiors? To rescue from barbarism the world that followed the inevitable war?

He could believe in a supreme entity—a being capable of injecting point and purpose into existence. He felt the presence of a plan now—he sensed his own significant role in the great design. The Superiors had been placed upon the Earth at the exact point in human history when they were needed, when their role was crystal clear.

Anna had said he should refuse to do their bidding, that he should convince the others to resist. He had considered such a course of action in the past, but now he knew better: in failing to act, he had in fact done right. When the war was over—that was the time to begin saying no. Then he would step forward and explain the situation and convince the other Superiors to follow his lead. Their vast powers would be put to use for the greater good not only of themselves but of the human race as well. It would work. They would listen to him. His past views would testify to the sincerity of his present position. His views would be accepted. But the war would have to come first.

He wished there were someone he could tell. But not Anna—he couldn't trust her to understand. And he didn't want to tell Sylvia because to tell her that much would necessitate telling her everything and he would never do that. And there was no one else—certainly not Astor nor the Circle. They sought power in order to subjugate the human race, not to help it.

But wouldn't time change that? He had to believe so. Time was the great transformer, the universal force with the ability to change anything.

He suddenly noticed that Anna was looking at him. The editing machine was dark.

"I—" She was trying to fight that barrier again, but

it was larger now. "There's something I want you to see." She stood up.

"What?"

"A program."

"Not that again."

She was desperately sincere. "No, it's real this time. I mean it. Eathen—tell him."

"Yes," Eathen agreed. He stood beside Anna, as if he were capable of providing her with firm support.

"All right." Alec shrugged. "I'll come.

The three of them—Anna in the lead—walked off into the garden.

eleven

The three of them—Anna, Eathen, Alec—went to the place in the garden where the two wooden benches sat facing each other. Alec occupied one bench and Anna the other. Eathen crouched down at her feet.

Slowly, deliberately, Anna said, "I want you to watch this, Alec. I think it may be very important."

"No tricks?"

"None," she said. "None at all."

"I still say—" Alec began but before he could finish the thought Anna and Eathen and the garden had disappeared. Instead, he was sitting among several thousand strangers in a huge, round, concrete stadium. Above, the sky was an odd shade of gray but otherwise unremarkable. There was a cold wind. The people were white-skinned, often blond, shabbily dressed. Their garments—ties and trousers and thick sweaters—had been out of fashion for decades. The wind caused everyone's hair to lean in one direction. The wind also seemed to sweep away any words. Around him, many lips were moving but he could hear nothing beyond a few, uncertain moans. He stared at the people closest to him, trying to make sense of their presence. Suddenly, out of the corner of an eye, he spied a familiar face:

84

Inspector Cargill.

He stood up, shouted, waved his hands. Cargill remained seated, his eyes turned toward the sunken center of the stadium. Alec started to move but his feet refused to budge. He remembered that this was a tape; his presence in this crowd was merely an illusion. But Cargill—that was no illusion. He was really here.

Suddenly, Alec's attention was drawn toward the center of the stadium. A wooden podium rested down there upon a small circle of artificial lawn. It was so far away he could not tell for certain if anyone was actually standing down there. But something had drawn his gaze—a flash of motion. There—he saw it again. The others did too. Abruptly, the crowd fell silent. Their lips ceased to move, the occasional moans stopped. All eyes were focused downward. Even the wind seemed to fade, as if it were waiting too. Then, from below, an amplified voice spoke. Alec groaned aloud.

The voice was Ah Tran's:

It said:

"Tonight, my lovers, young and old, I have chosen as my subject not godly things but rather human events. I wish to speak to you of the history of our race, but when I use that word—history—I do not desire you to think of an inexorably rising tide commencing with the establishment of so-called civilization and sweeping onward past such now submerged landmarks as Babylon, Egypt, the Indus Valley, Athens, Rome, the T'ang dynasty, Byzantine, the Golden Horde, the Mayans and Incas and Aztecs, the Spanish and French and British empires, the American Domination, Soviet Russia, and so on up to our present, precarious two-state world. Nor do I even wish you to think in scientific rather than political terms: from Democritus through Euclid, Archimedes, Ptolemy, Al-Khowarizmi, Galileo, Kepler, Francis Bacon, Newton, Gauss, Clausius, Darwin, Planck, Albert Einstein, Alec Richmond, and so on. Or the arts: poetry, epic, novel, painting, sculpture, music, filmmaking. I see no need to bore you with the sounding of further names. Or even—my own specialty—prophecy, theology: Moses,

Lao-Tze, Buddha, Confucius, Jesus, Mohammed, Mao, and their latter day interpreters, disciples, corrupters. To see history in these terms—in any terms of mere progression—is to ignore the central question: Which is greater? Superior? Was the civilization of twentieth century America greater than that of the Kingdom of Axum? Was Milton a greater poet than Homer? Which is it? Can you say? Greater? Lesser? Or—and I place my name with those who here cry *Aye!*—different? Let us continue, carrying this question of progression onward into absurdity. Einstein a greater scientist than Archimedes? Mahler a greater composer than Bach? Rossellini a greater filmmaker than John Ford? Anna Richmond a greater artist than François Auguste Rodin? Myself a greater prophet than the Buddha? I reply to these questions—and they are not intended wholly rhetorically—you may substitute any names you wish—I reply with a laugh."

And he laughed—long, loud, sharp.

Swiftly, he raised a hand and silenced the applause.

"Please—no—wait!" he cried. "Permit me to finish, then express your pleasure. The point I wish to make is simply that the sheer, steep line of history is a myth. It does not exist. The truth is less complex and more complete. It lies—" he raised a hand (in spite of the distance, Alec could clearly see) and drew a circle in the air "—here. A closed line. A circle, repeating itself endlessly. So it is with the universe, with the individual man, and so it must also be with history itself. It is a cycle and not some mad slope of a mountain effortlessly rising infinitely higher until even the gods must laugh at the silliness and awkwardness of the conception.

"A child is born nameless. Soon, he is provided by his makers with a firmer identity and is sent forth to view and experience the world. Yet the child is no greater at twenty years than he was at twenty months. When old age strikes, that is not a matter of declining, either. Remember: I speak to you not of the parabola but rather of the circle. As we grow old, this is the truth of our experience: the circle is simply closing—as

86

it must. The result—inevitably—is death, the repetition of birth.

"So it is with the individual man and so, too, is it with the universe man inhabits. In the beginning, matter existed, we are told, as a finite speck of awesome density. The result was an explosion of incredible power. The universe was thus shattered and born in a real sense, rushing outward to fill the void with light and life. But was this all? Will it end here? No, for we are also told that gravity will eventually gain control. The universe will contract. That dense, finite speck will be reborn. And the result—once more—the mighty bang. Again, we glimpse the existence of the circle. The cycle which can neither end nor begin.

"The universe. The individual man. And what of nature, you may ask. What of evolution? Hasn't mankind evolved from forgotten ancestors who once roamed the plains of Africa? Survival of the fittest—we have heard this expression used endlessly to describe our plight. The process of weeding out, the separation of the fit from the unfit. In coming here today, did any of us have to take care to avoid the roving herds of Triceratops? When did any of us last see a living Mammoth or, for that matter, a Neanderthal? All of these creatures—gone, dead, extinct, unfit. And so, common knowledge has proclaimed, it is the same with history. Civilization also evolves. Failed conceptions are weeded out. Man struggles but he also rises. He ascends ever upward toward ... toward ... what ...?

"I deny this attitude. I call it a desecration. A parallel based upon truth—yes—but transformed—through the means of falsehoods of omission—into a lie. I do not deny evolution. Rather, I prefer to proclaim ecology. Not only natural selection but also natural balance. The circle." Again, he drew the symbol in the air. "The cycle. Here is history's real metaphor. The purpose of evolution—it is not as some believe an end to itself—has been to perfect the ecosystem. The purpose of history has been to perfect the human ecosystem—our own intraspecies ecosystem—the relation of individual man to man—in other words, civilization.

We have progressed—I dare to use that term—inexorably toward a meaningful system of mutualism within ourselves. And while I do proclaim the possibility of perfection, I reject the conception that this is something new. Civilization, rather obviously, has existed since the dawn of civilization. Therefore, the cycle has too. The failure has been ours in failing to detect its presence. At my school in the Andes Mountains, my most brilliant disciples, laboring for many years, have succeeded in devising a series of illustrated charts that indicate and describe exactly how this mutualism exists in contemporary society. All of us have seen charts of the carbon and nitrogen cycles, of food chains and so forth. Come to me and I will show you the cycle of civilization itself.

"So, knowledge is ours. We may no longer plead mere ignorance. But what of wisdom, which knowledge may grant but never require? If we are truly wise, I say, now is the moment to turn in fear. I speak to you of the possibility of rupture. It is a thing I fear more than Satan himself, for the two are one and the same—they share the same face. I wish to warn you of a great dark slouching beast come to rend the fabric of our frail mutualism." His voice began to rise, not shouting but rather chanting. Alec felt certain there were tears in his eyes. (But how could he know that?) "We must beware. We must be vigilant. We must protect ourselves, for if this beast slips past our careless gaze and moves beyond and behind us, it will turn and destroy us with savage unconcern. I warn you. I beg and implore you. My children—brothers, sisters, lovers—my fellow human beings—*beware!*"

With that, the image faded. The stadium was no more. Alec sat in the garden. Anna and Eathen faced him.

Alec whispered, "He knows."

"What?" said Anna, who had not heard.

"About us. He knows. That was what he meant. The whole speech was about us. The cycle—it excludes us. The great slouching beast—it is us."

88

"No," said Anna, shaking her head as if possessed of a deeper and darker knowledge.

"Yes," Alec insisted. "He mentioned both our names. How did he know? He called me a scientist. The android project is supposed to be secret. If he knows about that, he might know about anything. And Cargill—I saw him there too."

"Inspector Cargill is a disciple," Eathen said.

"What?" demanded Alec, turning on the android.

But Anna stepped between them. She held up a hand, shielding Eathen, protecting him from Alec. "No," she said. "Go away. Let him alone."

"But I—" For the first time, Alec realized that the android was radiating. The emotion he received was so powerful that he was unable to continue: fear—deep, dark, total, overwhelming fear. "I'm sorry," he said.

Anna said nothing. She crouched above Eathen, speaking softly to him.

Alec waited, then turned his back on them both, striding away between the dark trees. He made no attempt to glance back.

twelve

It was far too cold out here for taking a walk. Alec had neglected to grab a coat when leaving the house and was now actually shivering from the chill. The sensible thing, if he wanted to do it, would be to turn right around this moment and hurry back to home and heat and bed. Sensible—yes—but he knew he wasn't going to do it. Sensibility was a state of mind that existed far beyond his present ability to accept. His feet kept moving—without conscious volition. Each additional step was a separate and individual motion. One—then another—and another. And, all this time, the house dwindled farther into the distance.

Then he turned a corner on the path and couldn't see the house anymore. He was quite alone at last.

Alec wasn't walking anyplace in particular. He neither possessed nor sought any definite destination. He was following the path down to the hovercraft terminal but didn't actually expect to reach that point. Fortunately, the path was quite well lighted. That would force any wild animals that might be lurking in the surrounding woods to keep their distance. Wild animals were afraid of light. But—wild animals? Here? White light shined down from the lowest branches of the trees. Wires ran along both sides of the path, linking the individual lights into a mass. The forest was otherwise thick and impenetrable. There weren't any wild animals out here. Men had driven them away centuries ago.

Why was he out here? He had come as soon as he left Anna and Eathen in the garden. Wasn't there supposed to be a reason for this aimless walk? Ah—he remembered—it was so he could think. Well, he didn't want to think. What was there to think about? Anna? She was leaving him. The war? It was coming. Ah Tran? Eathen? Cargill? Sylvia? Work? The Inner Circle

That was what was wrong. There was too much to think about. He could walk twice around the world—superior mentality or not—and never complete all his thoughts.

So he might as well go back home. That would be the sensible course. Yes. He had definitely made up his mind to do just that—only a few more steps—when, from the high woods to the left of the trail, he heard a low, anguished sound, a moan, like an animal in pain.

But there weren't any animals out here.

He stopped, extending his senses outward, sweeping the woods. He stood stock still. But, no—nothing. Then it must be an animal, no matter what, for animals do not radiate. But the moan had not sounded like any cry that an animal would choose to make.

He was more than ready to go home now. He had actually begun to retrace his steps when the moan sounded again. There was a brief pause—silence—and then it came again. This time, it did not stop.

It was human. Yes. No animal could make that cry. Only a man could suffer that much.

He called out, "Who's there?" and stepped to the side of the path, following the sound of the moaning. He stepped away from the light. The woods swallowed him up. He couldn't see his feet. He tried to move confidently but stumbled almost at once, sprawling on his face. Quickly, he regained his feet, plunging forward. Squinting, he strained to penetrate the darkness. He pushed a clump of ferns aside and trudged ahead. The ground was very damp, as if following a heavy rain. Deep, unexpected pockets of mud grasped at his shoes. The ground made an ugly, sucking noise when he pulled his feet away from it. He could hear crickets singing peaceably. A flock of mosquitoes buzzed near his head. The moaning kept on—a continuous sound.

"Are you all right? I'm coming. Can't you hear?"

Such questions seemed senseless—ridiculous—but the casual sound of his own voice was reassuring. Finally, after a dozen yards of desperate, blind thrashing, he reached a narrow, snug trail. He stopped and listened. The moaning seemed to be coming from off to the left—not too far—perhaps another dozen yards. He turned that way, keeping cautiously to the trail. He thought it amazing the way, when you entered an apparently untrodden stretch of woods, there always seemed to be fresh trails to follow. How did the trails get there? Who or what made them? And why?

His eyes were growing more accustomed to the dark. Wasn't it ironic that, as a Superior, he had been granted exceptional sensory abilities only in impractical ways? Why not superior vision or hearing or touch? Why did it have to be limited to the interior mind—to a painful, barely useful sort of empathy? He thought, *We are incomplete supermen,* but that glib phrase no longer seemed to be enough. *We are accursed with this superiority.* Wasn't that closer to the truth?

He paused. The moaning was very close now. He listened sharply, depending wholly upon the information provided by his ears. The sound emanated from off the trail. This way. Using his hands, he searched the edge of the path, seeking an outlet. Ah. Here was a hole. Ducking down, he stepped carefully through a large gap in the foliage. A shallow recession. The moaning definitely came from here. It burned in his ears.

Reaching into his trouser pockets, he found a few old kitchen matches. Not many. Enough, he hoped. He lit one. The dim glow barely penetrated the darkness. He stared at the ground, moving in a circle, searching for some sign. The moaning seemed to come from everyplace at once—he couldn't follow it.

A shoe. Ah. Reaching down, he grabbed it up. The match flickered out. He held the shoe close to his face. It seemed incredibly heavy. No wonder—the foot was still in it. The body, however, was not—no, just the foot. His hands were all sticky. Blood. Pints and quarts and gallons of blood. He gagged. The moaning droned on. The sound seemed to be coming from the severed foot. He hurled the shoe far, far away into the dark depths of the woods.

He lit a second match and forced himself to press more deeply ahead. He found the body—what remained of it—and crouched down. The match went out as he moved. He did not care to light another. He could see quite well enough. He placed his face close to the one on the body's head and squinted. Small eyes—dark—open. Skin that was barely discernible— dark—black. A Negro!

That explained it. No wonder there hadn't been any radiations. Alec saw that he had made an error. This wasn't any man. Of course, it wasn't an animal either. It was Timothy Ralston—a Superior.

"Oh, no!" Alec cried, letting the face go, backing off.

Ralston had sensed Alec's approach along the path and erected a shield around his pain. It was a wise gesture, for Alec did not think he would ever be able to come this far otherwise. Ralston must be suffering horribly, as much—no, more (Ralston was a Superior)—than Mencken that other time.

With numb fingers, Alec searched under his arm.

But he should have remembered: he didn't have the gun any more. Having used it once, he had disposed of it. If he wanted to help Ralston now, he would have to find cruder, less delicate means. But first there was something he wished to try. He lit another match and focused the glow directly on Ralston's lips.

"Tim, can you tell me who did this to you?"

Ralston's lips parted. They seemed to move. But no sound came out.

"Who?" Alec repeated. "Was it them, the others?"

Ralston nodded his head—once—sharply. But the gesture seemed to consume all his remaining energies. His eyes—which had been open until then—fell shut; he cried out in pain.

The match was very warm against Alec's fingers. He asked—quickly: "Did you know him? The one who did this? His name?"

Ralston nodded—yes—but again cried out. The match singed Alec's fingers and he dropped the stub.

If there were only some way. But there wasn't. If Ralston let down the shield and opened his mind to radiate, then his pain would simply pour out, overwhelming everything rational. If they wanted to communicate, they would have to talk. But could they? What if the one who had done this had also cut out Ralston's tongue or severed his vocal cords?

Alec moved his hands through the moist dirt below his knees, seeking the object he now required. He found one large rock but it felt much too smooth, like an egg. He crawled farther away, fingering the earth as he moved, and finally found exactly what he needed: a big, sharp, jagged rock.

He came back to Ralston's side and laid the rock close to his face.

"Tim—look here."

Ralston's eyes moved. Alec could see that much. It no longer seemed quite as dark here as before. He glanced up. Directly overhead, the moon was shining.

"I want you to try and tell me. Then I'll do it. But first you have to tell. Understand?"

Ralston nodded.

"Can you talk at all?"

A headshake: *no*.

"Then—tell me—was it Cargill?"

No.

"My wife—Anna?"

No.

"But it was someone I know?"

Yes.

"A Superior?"

No.

"Was it—?" He tried to think of another name. While he knelt there, Ralston suddenly shut his eyes. Alec shied back. Dimly, he could sense it coming. He clenched his hands and moaned with expectation. The barrier was falling. Now Ralston moaned too, a wail which grew louder and louder. Alec screamed as the anguish ripped through his mind. His hands flew up, the jagged rock clenched in between. He brought the rock down. *Crash*. Up—down. He couldn't stop. His own brain was on fire. Up—down. Again and again. He couldn't stop until—all at once—the pain vanished.

That meant Ralston was dead.

Alec fell across the body of his friend and lay there, panting, gasping, spent.

At last, he staggered back to his feet, breathing hard. He realized he was still holding the rock. He didn't want it. He dropped it. *Thud*. The dead sound sickened him. He turned, trying to run, fell to his knees, then clawed his way back to the trail. Then he was able to stand upright again. He ran. Branches reached out and tore at his clothes. He veered off the trail a dozen times, falling, banging into trees or bushes, scraping his knees and hands, cutting his face. At last the path seemed to widen. He had reached the main trail. The lights shining down from the trees blinded him momentarily. He stumbled but caught himself before he fell. He laughed. He couldn't let himself stop now. No, sir. If he did that, he would never get started again. The house must be right ahead. He could almost see it. Full of sudden hope, he ran like a demon.

94

Eventually, he crashed into the front door. His fingers trembling from the effort, he let himself in. The house seemed peculiarly dark and silent. Tentatively, he called:

"Eathen? Anna?"

He tiptoed down the corridor. A light was shining under Anna's door. He pressed his ear against the wood. From inside, he clearly heard voices. One was Anna and—yes—the other voice was Anna too. Her words were not clear.

He drew back. Did he want to see Anna? What could he say to her? That it had happened again—that it had been worse this time than before?

He moved down the corridor and went silently into his study. He dropped into a chair and sat there a long time, staring at the palms of his hands, studying all the blood he saw there. Whose was it? His? Or Ralston's?

After a time, he became aware that the phone was ringing. He got up slowly and padded toward the living room. The light under Anna's door was gone. He did not stop to make sure she was sleeping.

By the time he reached the phone, Eathen had appeared from someplace and answered it. Alec glanced past the android and saw Sylvia Mencken's face reflected on the viewscreen.

"Is it for me?" he asked.

Eathen nodded. He was staring at Alec.

"Then let me have it." Alec came forward. His gaze met Eathen's directly—and locked. Suddenly, Alec realized that Eathen was radiating. He struggled to discover the meaning of this emotion. Then he had it: pity.

He shoved Eathen aside and grabbed the phone.

"Hello," he said.

PART
TWO
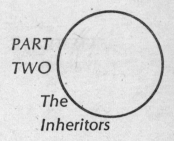
The
Inheritors

Karlton Ford sat in a wicker chair in the center of a flat, green, clover-infested meadow. His eyes were focused upon the clean blue sky. A white cloud drifted into his line of sight. In shape, the cloud perfectly resembled the figure of a mounted, charging horseman, sword raised in preparation for combat. As the cloud moved, the feet of the horse also moved, matching the motions of a galloping stallion. Ford observed the passing cloud sculpture with a fixed, analytic expression. When the cloud reached a point directly overhead, he frowned and looked down at the trampled grass beneath him.

"I don't like it, McCoy," he said.

"Yes, sir," said a tiny voice, which seemed to emanate from underground.

"I mean now," said Ford, glancing up. The horse and rider continued to drift across the surface of the sky.

"Yes, sir!"

When he glanced up again, all sign of the cloud was gone. He smiled and said:

"That's better."

"Anything else, sir?" asked the voice.

"Oh, I don't know. Is the news ready?"

"Yes, sir."

Ford leaned back in the chair and scratched his chin. He sighed loudly. "All right—give me the news."

"But, sir, I thought—"

He sat up rigidly. "What was that, McCoy?"

"Your daughter, sir. I think she—"

"Don't," Ford said. He was breathing heavily. "I don't want you ever to do that. Don't think, McCoy."

"But she's awake, sir."

"Feed her."

"And after that?"

99

"Tell her—oh, tell her I'll be there in a minute. I want to watch the news first."

"I'll roll it, sir."

"Do that."

Ford sighed. Dull, dull, dull. That was the only handicap of being so rich that anything you wanted they ran and got it before you could ask: you got bored. Nothing was ever exciting; anticipation was a lost emotion.

He looked up at the sky but it remained blank and blue. McCoy was slow today. Inefficiency bored Karlton Ford, and what bored him always irritated him, and what he found irritating, he soon grew to hate. He ought to warn McCoy. The little man had a good job here. He ought not to risk losing it through lack of initiative.

But maybe the problem was simply technical. The sky was still blank. Even McCoy was not that stupid.

The voice from underground suddenly said, "I'll have it for you in a minute, sir."

Ford grunted. Near his chair, a herd of cows munched contentedly on the high grass. The cows were spotted black and white but, in spite of the fact that he was one of the world's ten largest suppliers of natural milk, he didn't know one breed of dairy cattle from another. Perhaps an acre farther away—on the opposite side of a low barbed fence—a handful of horses drank from a narrow stream. Ford owned all of this—stream, horses, cattle, sky, clouds, McCoy. Anything within sight of his present vantage point, he owned—and a great deal more besides. Besides this ranch here in Wyoming, he owned a house in New York State—along the Hudson River—and apartments in Geneva, Tokyo, and Honolulu. He wasn't the richest man in the world; he was the third richest. But the other two were men exactly like himself. He was a private person. Fewer than twenty men had ever met him face-to-face. Under his present identity, that is; at other times, he had been more free and personable. In his life, he had used a variety of names. James Henry Walsh was one. As Karlton Ford, he was rich, powerful, and feared. Also, though this was far from common knowledge, he was a superman.

The day's news began to appear against the surface of the sky, the events of the past few hours recreated in stunning, three-dimensional replica. Ford watched, vaguely intrigued. Here was the interior of the supposed atomic bomb plant in Borneo. Small, stooped, menacing, yellow-skinned men and women darting like bugs around the egg-shaped bomb. The scene was so ridiculous he didn't see how it could fool anyone. But it did—it fooled almost everyone. When he watched the news, Ford never allowed a commentator's sound-track to intrude. He didn't need anyone to explain the significance of events to him. If any particular item was really important, he already knew about it. The same was true of the next shot—a battalion of identical soldiers marching briskly across a barren field. The android army. Secret maneuvers. Preparing, if necessary, to move. Ford smiled. Then came scenes of actual fighting—sporadic incidents so far. Brief skirmishes in China, Mexico, Turkey. A bombed-out village—somewhere in Indonesia—Java, he recalled. An attempt by the civilized nations to knock out the bomb works. A failure, of course—predestined, since the bomb itself was a hoax. Then came brief shots of the various so-called leaders of the world. Talking, talking, talking. Endlessly droning their pitiful cliches. He was glad he didn't have to hear. He felt more genuine contempt for these supposed leaders than he did for the race itself. One did not expect anything exceptional from ordinary men; one did at times hope to uncover some hidden spark in a leader. Ford had known several of these leaders, however, and the spark had always been absent. Like their followers, the leaders lacked ability, imagination, foresight, and intelligence. A war was coming. All of them—civilized and primitive alike—wished to avoid the conflict. Yet, in spite of this unanimity, they would fail. To Ford, it was a sad, sad joke.

The rest of the news failed to hold even his occasional attention. An editorial—apparently a government spokesman—Ford followed the speaker's lips sufficiently long to determine that the man was simply reciting a long and involved threat. The stock market continued to do surprisingly well—especially in those areas most directly related to Ford's own financial interests. He manufactured munitions. And sports. He decided to watch this part keenly. The sight of long-legged, half-naked boys and girls racing across fields and kicking round balls caused him to laugh aloud. Even with war only days away, they continued to play their games.

But, in a way, that was merely part of the one human characteristic he admitted admiring; their perseverance. If that was a virtue—their stubbornness—then the race surely possessed it. After all, for more than fifty years mankind had survived when, by all proper calculations, they should have collapsed and perished. Fifty years, Ford thought, since the first of us reached maturity. And we haven't won yet, he reminded himself. Although we will—we must—the time is finally here.

They called themselves the Inheritors, meaning the name as both boast and threat. When the human race fell—a matter of days, weeks—the Earth would be theirs. The earliest of the Inheritors—Ford was one of these—had been born some seventy years ago. They did not consider themselves mutants. They were supermen only in the sense of being superior, for they were not really men at all. Ford thought—and most Inheritors agreed—that they must be the children of some awesome extraterrestrial race which, for reasons of its own, had sent seed spores drifting across space. Whether the arrival of these spores on Earth was deliberate could not, of course, be determined; but sometimes Ford had a dream in which, after conquering Earth, he and the other Inheritors one day looked up into the sky and saw a fleet of starships coming down to rest; the ships, of course, carried their ancestors. But that was just a dream. The actual truth remained unknown. All Ford knew was that one day he had awakened inside the womb of a woman. A short time later, he had caused himself to be born. At twelve, he had left his temporary home and ventured into the world. By the time he turned fourteen, he had established contact with five other Inheritors. Ten years later, more than a hundred were known to each other. The first generation had ended there, but sons and daughters had soon followed. Now there were nearly three hundred Inheritors and new grandchildren were being born almost every week.

"Sir?" said the voice from the ground.

Frowning, Ford glared at the grass; "Now what, McCoy?"

"The news is over, sir."

"I know that."

"I mean Anna—your daughter, that is. She keeps asking me when you're coming."

"And what are you telling her?"

"I said you were on your way."

Ford smiled. "And is that true? Do I look as if I'm presently on my way?"

"Well, no, sir."

"Then you admit you lied? To your employer's daughter? Consciously? With deliberate malice?"

"Well . . . I—I. . . ."

"I think I'll take pity on you, McCoy. I know I ought to fire you but—well, I did say I'd pity you. And I do. So you may tell Anna that I will be there very shortly."

"Yes, sir."

"And next time, McCoy, don't be so eager."

"Yes, sir."

Sighing, Ford raised his eyes. The sky was blue and bare. He did not especially look forward to seeing Anna again. He was beginning to think the decision to allow her to establish contact had not been wise. Still, at the time, it had seemed necessary, especially with that ridiculous policeman sniffing at his old past trails. Better to tell her than to be found out. Less dangerous. And she might—because of her husband's essential role in their general designs—prove useful at some future time. And she did amuse him. He recalled her

103

mother with some warmth too. That incident had occurred during a period when—as protective camouflage—the Inheritors had taken human wives and husbands. The Superiors had been born then. A few of the marriages even continued to this date but, as soon as the first child was born, the relationship was always severed. It would not be wise to allow the Superiors to know the truth too soon—what they really were. Better to desert the children and kill the human mother or father. Ford thought he must have been soft. It had come from too close contact with humans for too long a time. That was why he had failed to place Anna in a government home; he had left her with human friends. When the fact was discovered, he had been forced to fight with all his might to keep the other Inheritors from censuring him. He had been made to admit a public mistake. Now he even had to live with that mistake—Anna was here.

Still, he would enjoy seeing her face. When she found out the truth. When the war ended and humanity was beaten and it was time for the final move. Checkmate. Then Anna—and her fellow Superiors—would discover what they really were—the hybrid children of truly superior creatures. Crippled, useless forms. Like mules. It would shatter them. Their lives, he knew were predicated upon delusions of superiority. None would survive a dose of the truth. A pity. But, once the war was over, their purpose in life would be ended anyway.

McCoy's shrill, piping voice interrupted his thoughts: "Sir, I hate to—"

"I'm coming!" Ford bellowed.

He stood up. Raising both hands above his head, he stamped a foot on the ground. Instantly, with a loud roar, he soared into the air. The tiny jets concealed in his tunic lifted him easily through the sky. He flew over the cattle, sped past the horses, hurried along the length of the stream. At last, in the distance, the high stone turrets of the castle came into view.

Here was home.

fourteen

She wasn't wearing a stitch but that didn't prevent the funny little man whose name she could hardly ever remember from popping his head through the door and saying as excitedly as a child on its birthday: "He's on his way, Anna."

She made no effort to cover herself. It didn't seem necessary or appropriate for McCoy—yes, sometimes she could remember, that was his name. She waved him inside, then looked away. McCoy radiated a constant veneer of furious tension, but there was never anything below. He made her feel uncomfortable. It was as if he lacked any real depth, as though a large portion of himself had been burned away and left empty.

She was lying on the big bed, facing the window: "You told me that a half-hour ago."

"Ah, but this time—" she sensed him trying to circle the bed so that she would have to look him in the eye and, as a compromise, turned her head and faced him "—it's true." He made a glib motion, crossing his heart and grinning hugely. "I mean, I just talked to him." The last word was spoken with a feeling that bordered upon reverence.

"Then you can let me alone now."

"Until he comes," McCoy corrected, crisply.

"Yes—exactly. Until he comes. Now—please—go."

"Yes, Anna." But he didn't move. He stood there, silently wringing his hands.

"Well, what?" she said, irritated.

"I wanted you to know." His grin grew even larger. "The sculpture equipment has arrived. I had it set up in the—"

"No," she said, sharply.

"But—"

"I told you I wasn't interested. I'm through, retired. I never want to see a strip of tape again in my life."

"But your talent. You don't know." He was shaking his head fiercely. "If you'd only just try one so that—"

"So that I could give it to you?" She sat up and glared at him. McCoy was a collector. He already owned several of her original tapes.

"I don't care about that. No. I just want your talent—I don't want it to be lost to the world."

"Oh, leave me alone," she said, with feeling.

"But—"

"I'll talk to you later." It was the only way of getting rid of him. "Maybe I will do something."

"Do you promise?"

"I promise we can talk about it."

"Oh, fine. That's enough—enough." He began to back out of the room, almost bowing, his smile firmly in place. "After you're through—through with him."

"Yes," she said.

"Oh, good. Oh, good."

She stood, stepped forward, and kicked the door shut. She sighed and shook her head. Then she went to the closet and grabbed a handful of clothes and threw them on. Turning, she glanced out the window.

From here, she could see very little besides the swimming pool and a corner of the garden. The pool was filled and emptied daily, but except for herself she had never seen anyone make use of it. While she watched, two servants crossed her line of sight. There seemed to be hundreds of them throughout the house, each identical to the others. For all the personality any of them exhibited, they could have been androids.

It was hard getting used to this life: she had never been this rich before. The bedroom, for instance, a huge chamber, was covered with paintings. She could identify most of the artists with considerable ease. The majority were old masters—on one wall alone, neatly arranged, were miniatures of Chagall, Renoir, Lichtenstein, and Klee. There was a massive Pollock too—undoubtedly an original—on the ceiling. In fact, it was the ceiling. But what disturbed Anna about these paintings was not their value but rather the lack of meaning and pattern to them taken as a whole. The

106

paintings were uniformly masterpieces but they did not mesh. It was as if the artist or school was insignificant as long as the work itself was valuable. The contemporary work, most of it by unknown artists, impressed her similarly. She somehow formed the distinct impression that, in a few years time, without exception, all of these paintings would be considered valuable masterpieces.

The bookshelves only confirmed her impression. One half of a wall was covered with first editions. All were well-known books—most were novels. At a glance, she noted *Middlemarch, The Princess Casamassima, Howard's End, The Red and the Black, An American Tragedy, Tender Is the Night, Kim.* While it was hardly impossible for one man to appreciate such a variety of authors—from Stendhal through James to Kipling and Fitzgerald—it was the manner in which the books were bound that served as her confirmation. Each was bound in uniform scarlet, with gold-leaf lettering. Which meant that the original bindings had been removed, thus reducing the books considerably in value. Didn't that indicate that Ford placed orderliness above authenticity? Or did it simply mean that extreme wealth permitted a person to ignore common attitudes toward value?

But did it matter? She turned away from the books and flopped on the bed. After all, she was a Superior and Ford, no matter how rich, was not. She had determined that during her first meeting with him. It had been, she admitted, a severe disappointment, but she had grown to like him since, even if he was only a human. In person, he was cold and undemonstrative, but his radiations were the opposite—warm and kindly. He was her real father and, if it hadn't been for the awe she felt at the splendiferous mode of life he followed, they might actually have become real friends once the barrier of his diffidence was penetrated. Still, she didn't understand all of it. This house—it was more like a castle than any regular home—the servants, the grounds. She had always been told that taxes had long ago rendered such brazen displays of wealth impossible. Millionaires were supposedly an extinct breed. The richest men of today were no better off than a moderately well-off man a century ago. If that was true—she laughed—those men of the past must have lived like a bunch of gods in heaven. And Ford lived alone too. All of this for one man alone. During her stay here, she had never met anyone except the servants. If Ford had friends, she had seen and heard no evidence of their existence. He never talked of anyone except him and her, and his thoughts—as she received them—were similarly empty of any outside, human interests. She didn't understand this part at all. In fact, there was a great deal about Ford that seemed to lie just beyond her ability to comprehend. She didn't know—had never asked—exactly how he had managed to acquire and then maintain his fortune.

Nor had he ever really explained his failure to search for her. When she had phoned that first time— struggling to penetrate a thick veil of secretaries and receptionists, automated and otherwise, until at last reaching McCoy at the ranch and then, with little explanation required, Ford himself—he hadn't seemed surprised. She told him about Cargill but he didn't seem to care. He had asked her at once to come to the ranch. And she had. But when, the first evening, she had tried to explain her reasons for wanting to find him, he had carefully changed the subject.

The door popped open. A face peeped through. McCoy, again, grinning. "He's here now, Anna."

"Oh, fine." She got off the bed and straightened her dress. "Please tell him I'll be right there."

Ford awaited her in the living room, a dark cavern so vast and ornate as to defy any attempt to describe it briefly. As she crossed the room, Anna heard the sound of her bare feet amplified enormously, so that the patter seemed to fill the whole room. Ford sat in a chair. She dropped at his feet, smiling. He radiated a calm tranquility that succeeded in erasing her own tensions with ease.

"What are your plans?" he asked, after a considerable silence between them.

"I'm not sure."

"Will you want to return to San Francisco soon?"

"I should."

"Your husband?"

"I don't know. I think he'd have me back if I came and got on my knees and cried and begged him."

"But you wouldn't do that."

"No, never."

"And you still haven't told him?"

"About you?" She smiled again, trying to reassure him; she knew how important to him his privacy was. "Of course not. I've hardly talked to him—"

"You called him last night."

"But—" How did he know that? McCoy. Of course. She had asked McCoy to place the call. She shook her head. "He thinks I'm visiting old friends in this area. He doesn't know anything about you. I promise."

"I believe you," he said, and the intensity of his faith moved her deeply.

"I'm glad."

"But you do like it here?"

"Oh, I—" she thought she ought to consider before answering the question, but the reply escaped her lips before she could begin to think "—I love it."

"Then why don't you stay here for good? I can see that your husband is notified that you have decided not to return to him."

"I'll call him."

"No, I don't think you should. I can take care of it more efficiently. There isn't anyone else, is there?"

"Anyone who would miss me?" This time she did consider. "No, not a soul. But are you sure you want me?"

"Yes. Besides the obvious reasons—you are my daughter and we have seen little or nothing of each other for decades—the international situation worries me. If war does come—and it may be any day now—I think you'll be safer here. This ranch is very well defended."

"Do you really think there'll be a war?"

"Don't you want one?"

In spite of the serenity he radiated, the question disturbed her deeply. Sometimes, like now, he seemed to say something that struck remarkably close to the truth. The one thing she never wanted him to know was that his daughter was a freak, a creature capable of listening to his private feelings and emotions. He had no idea of who or what she was, and she was determined to keep him ignorant. "Should I?" she asked, softly.

"I don't know. I don't even know how I ought to feel. War is a dreadful act, but right now, it seems to me that one can only clear the air."

"If we win."

"Yes. But I'm sure we will. These androids."

"I know all about them," she said, blurting out the words before thinking. "Alec designed them."

"Oh, did he?" But Ford did not seem overly interested, as if he already knew, though this was the first time Anna had mentioned Alec's work.

"Yes, he did. But do you know what's really funny? The androids are all supposed to be so stupid and dense. Well, Alec brought the prototype home and made him our servant—I named him Eathen—spelling it in a funny way so that nobody would think he was human—and Eathen turned out to be completely different. He even managed to develop real emotions, feelings."

"He what?" Ford seemed disturbed. For the first time, the cold, placid mask of his face flickered with real emotion.

"He learned to laugh and cry and be happy and sad. I taught him to appreciate music and painting and literature. He's gone now but, for a time, near the end, we were very close."

"And where is he now?" Ford asked, coldly.

"Maybe I didn't put it right," she said, hoping to ease his anger by backtracking a bit. But what was wrong with him? Some common prejudice she didn't know about? What was wrong with an android developing emotions if it could? She thought Eathen's transformation a remarkable and wonderful achieve-

110

ment. "I mean, the feelings had to be there first. I didn't just—"

"I asked," Ford said, "where the android is now."

She felt embarrassed saying it, as if the truth were an admission of her own failure. "He joined the Ah Tran movement. He's a disciple, I understand. He lives in their community in Southern California."

Ford's mouth dropped open. His face flushed with anger. He leaped to his feet and commanded: "Stay here!"

She jumped up with him, crying, "But, I didn't—"

"Stay!" he shouted.

Ford charged past her. To avoid being knocked down, she fell to the side. His anger—and fear—she was certain of that now too—sprang out, gripping her so powerfully she was frozen. And her head was on fire. She cried out. Her brain was exploding. Lying on the floor, she trembled as if caught in some massive tremor of the earth. Distantly, she heard a door slam. Then she was screaming. For she had glimpsed something else: a thing so monstrous, ugly, foul that there was no way of comprehending its reality beyond screaming and screaming and screaming.

She had seen the truth reflected in his mind: she knew who Karlton Ford was, and what.

An instant later, it was gone—forgotten. Lying on the floor, she shook her head dimly. The pain gone, she sat up and blinked furiously. What was she doing here? Then she recalled that Ford had left and asked her to stay and wait. But she felt strangely weak, as if she had just suffered through some tremendous ordeal.

She made herself stand up. Across the room, thin twisting streams of sunlight came pouring through the few high slanting windows, sweeping across the floor in yellow waves. But it seemed cold. She was actually shivering. Hugging herself, she paced the room. Waiting for her father to come back home.

fifteen

Whenever possible, Eathen liked to leave the monastery at dusk and step out on the lawn and sit down and watch the sun as it slowly fell into the sea. He had to be especially careful while doing this. He had been created with a powerful immunity to pain and there was always the chance he would become so involved watching the spectacle that he would not turn his eyes away in time and thus blind himself.

So today, watching the sun, he wore a pair of thick dark glasses and frequently glanced away from the big orange disk as it continued its inexorable descent into the richly painted waves. Behind him, the big white house—the monastery—climbed upwards toward the sky. Eathen turned and looked back there. He wondered why Ah Tran insisted the house be called the monastery. In all his life, Eathen had never seen a house half so magnificent as this one. They were renting it. During more glorious times, it might well have served as a palace of kings or popes or presidents. Eathen, unlike some disciples, did not object to their living amid such splendor. At least he did not object for Ah Tran's part. He felt it proper that a man as great as the new messiah should have a residence to match his personal grandeur. Eathen and the other disciples were the ones who were not fit; it wasn't Ah Tran.

But it was difficult for Eathen here. He was an android, not a man, and no matter how many emotions he learned to feel, there was no changing the way in which he had been born. In the monastery, when one of the rented servants approached and addressed him as sir, he had to resist the urge to laugh or weep or grow violently angry. He wasn't a sir—he was a thing. An object made of flesh and blood. Ah Tran liked to call him Arthur instead of Eathen. He said the original Arthur had been a great king born of royal blood but required to wait for the right moment to assume his throne. Arthur had undergone testing, education, maturation before finally revealing his true nature Ah Tran showed Eathen a book in which there was a drawing of young King Arthur raising a sword from out of a stone. Ah Tran had remarked that Eathen might one day be expected to do something similar to prove his humanity. Eathen didn't know—he was afraid, when the moment of his test did come, that he would fail. He wasn't human—he was an android.

By the time Eathen remembered and looked back at the ocean, the sun was already gone. It seemed to happen this way quite often. Did California sunsets really happen faster than they did elsewhere? Or was this only another illusion? The most difficult part of learning how to be human, he was discovering, was knowing how to tell the difference between illusion and reality. For a long time he had suffered from the belief that anything seen, felt, or heard was real; he had accepted that the senses could not lie. Ah Tran, when Eathen expressed this belief, had laughed. Not only can they lie, the messiah had said, they very often do. Eathen was finding life composed of a complex set of complications.

He removed the dark glasses and cautiously rubbed his eyes. At the edge of the horizon, a pale purple streak could still be seen—a faint remnant of the sunset. So another day had come and gone and vanished. This tranquil life they were leading now—he and Ah Tran and the other disciples—was making him impatient. But wasn't that a good sign too? Impatience? Another human emotion? Didn't it signify that he was drawing ever closer to that central moment when his strength and wisdom would allow him to reach out and raise his own metaphorical Excalibur from the stone?

When he had first left Anna and joined Ah Tran, he had traveled around the world. He had stood beside the messiah in Moscow, Warsaw, Paris, London, New York, St. Louis, San Francisco—where he had seen Anna for the last time—Honolulu, Peking, Tokyo, Saigon, Sydney, Delhi. On several occasions—mostly near the end of the tour in Asia—he had been allowed to address the people himself. He had never alluded to his true nature—his androidism—and Ah Tran had told him that it wasn't necessary. All men were once boys, Ah Tran had said, but none consider it necessary to refer to their boyhood each time they perform a manly deed. "It must be the same with you, Arthur, and that is why you need not—and should not—refer to your condition."

"What did you call me?" he had asked. "Arthur?"

And that was when—in Tokyo, two months ago—Ah Tran had explained about his new name.

Now a servant approached from the house, a tiny black-skinned man dressed in gorgeous flowing linen robes.

"The messiah is prepared for you to receive him now," the servant said.

The careful phrasing of the sentence confused Eathen. "In his room, you mean?"

"No, sir. In yours."

"Ah Tran? In my room?" For a moment, he thought the servant was deliberately ridiculing him. "Are you certain?"

"I am, sir. He is there now."

Eathen shook his head. Such an event, if true, was simply astonishing. Among followers of Ah Tran, matters of ceremony and decorum were rigidly observed. Caste was an essential aspect of life, and Ah Tran occupied the uppermost stratum quite alone. Forms of address, table etiquette, greeting and farewells—all such manners of polite intercourse were firmly structured. No one ever spoke to Ah Tran until he spoke first. One always bowed when the messiah entered or left a room. And—when Ah Tran wished to speak to a disciple—it was expected, unless the matter was extremely urgent, that the disciple would go to see him.

"Is something wrong?" Eathen asked, already hurrying toward the house. "Is it an urgent matter?"

The servant, struggling to keep pace, said, "He told me to say that you may receive him at your convenience."

Eathen burst through the high front doors and dashed up the winding staircase three steps at a time. What could it be? Why had Ah Tran chosen to adopt the role of the suppliant? Was it something he—Eathen—had done?

His room, along with those occupied by the other two dozen disciples, was located in a single wing of the house. Ah Tran's quarters took up the entire upper, third story. The bathroom Ah Tran used—and bathing was a daily rite with them—was twice the size of Eathen's entire room.

When he reached the door to his room, he paused, then knocked gently and carefully—twice. When there was no immediate reply, he stepped back, prepared to wait. He did—time passed—but still nothing happened. Irritated, he turned to go find the servant and discover the meaning of this charade, but just then the door opened and a brown, glowing face appeared. Eathen blinked, deeply confused. Who was this? The man bowed his head, showing Eathen the crown of a smooth bald skull. The man was young, handsome, apparently an American Negro. The face appeared again, grinning. Suddenly, Eathen recognized the man. It was Ah Tran—but Ah Tran totally transformed. No longer was the messiah an old and infinitely wise denizen of the mysterious East—Tibet or Nepal, most believed. This man in front of him could have been any thirty-year-old Negro on the streets of New York.

His voice was different too. The frail, mystical accent had gone: "I am here to serve you, Arthur."

Unable to speak, Eathen nodded and carefully entered the room. Ah Tran bowed, waited until Eathen had passed, then shut the door.

Eathen stood in the middle of the small, austere room, seeking to find words worth speaking.

Ah Tran pointed shyly to the one piece of furniture the room contained: a high, stiff, straight-backed chair.

"Do you want me to sit there?" Eathen asked.

"The choice is yours, sir," said Ah Tran.

Eathen went over and sat on the chair. In a sudden, swift motion, Ah Tran dropped to the bare floor, crouching at Eathen's feet. He turned his eyes downward and made no effort to speak.

Eathen waited, slowly understanding what was expected of him, though not why. He was to speak first. But he had never done that before—how could he? Eathen cleared his throat, coughed, looked away.

Still, Ah Tran crouched silently and motionlessly.

At last, in a rush, Eathen said, "But you wished to see me, sir."

Ah Tran glanced up, his eyes darting furiously, as if he lacked the strength to meet Eathen's gaze. His smile was diffident. "I have prayed that you might listen to me, Arthur."

"But of course I will. When have I—?"

Ah Tran shook his head miserably. "You are far too kind." Eathen had to keep reminding himself that this weak, shaken young man was indeed the messiah.

"No—" Eathen began, but he interrupted himself, too confused to continue. This line of talk was solving nothing. "Please tell me whatever it is you want to say," he demanded, with a gruffness that shocked and frightened him.

But Ah Tran did not object. "I have been," he said, "an utter fool." Like any shame-faced penitent, he lowered his eyes. "My petty egotism has nearly shattered our best opportunity to achieve full success in our quest. Only a liar, idiot, shallow and foul beast could fail so miserably to uphold the faith of those who had placed their lives in his hands."

"But, messiah, surely you have not—" Again, Eathen interrupted himself.

"Ah, but I have. My name is Ah Tran—I cannot change that—but I am no messiah. A messiah is one who provides the opportunity of salvation for those who elect to follow his lead. In truth, I have failed to provide even for myself. I must speak of the activities of our circle. Even now, as shameful as the memory must be, I glimpse visions of our past. I see you—all of you—my most devoted disciples—gathered around. At the center of the circle, I sit alone. Your souls rush outward, fusing with mine, while I alone attempt the

116

awesome burden of sending this gestalt spinning toward the heavens. Again and again, the sacred effort miserably fails. I stand, cursing, wagging my finger like a tongue of retribution. In doing that—" he slapped the side of his head with a fist "—I have been a fool. The finger should have been turned upon myself. I was the one who had failed. I had dared to occupy—for no reason but sheer egotism—a seat that was not rightly mine to hold. The position of spiritual conduit should not have been granted a fool. Instead, it should have gone—" and now he did point, holding his finger steady, straight ahead, at Eathen "—to you."

"To me?"

Ah Tran smiled. "Exactly. I expected you might have known, but obviously your deep sense of personal humility has prevented you from exposing my crass idiocy. You expend too much pity on an old man. In truth, I have lived too long. My soul is cluttered with corruption and waste. My spiritual self—no different from any system that has existed too long—rushes toward a state of final disorganization. But you, Arthur, are barely a child. Your first conscious, waking moment occurred but months past. With you—" he grew excited, hands flashing in emphasis "—with you at our center, acting as spiritual conduit, I am convinced we shall succeed. You shall send us spinning upward. We shall reach the heavens, complete the cycle, learn the. . . ." His excitement faded as rapidly as it had come, he stopped, unable to continue.

"Yes?" said Eathen.

Ah Tran softly murmured, "If only you would agree. If you would just say yes. Grant us the privilege of your presence. Agree to endure the penetration of our fused souls. Then—I swear I believe it—we could . . . but—" he shrugged "—alas, you must refuse."

"I must? But, why should I?"

"Then you do not?"

"No, I—" Eathen said.

But Ah Tran did not give him a chance to finish. His face broke into a wide grin and, bounding up, he kissed Eathen warmly on the cheek. "You," he whispered,

117

"are the true messiah. From you and you alone, salvation will truly flow. I beg you now to grant me leave to depart so that I may communicate the glorious news to our brethren lovers."

"Of course," Eathen said. "But I'd like—"

"An hour," Ah Tran said, glancing at his watch. "We shall await you in my chambers. And don't be late. Please."

"No," Eathen said. "I'll be sure to—" Ah Tran was waiting. Eathen realized that their positions had once more been reversed. Quickly but carefully, he stood and bowed, bending stiffly at the waist. "Messiah," he murmured. "Your presence has honored me beyond compare."

"I thank you." Ah Tran bowed sharply, then turned and hurried to the door. He did not pause to say good-bye. In a bare moment, he was gone.

Eathen slumped back into the chair. I have been tricked, he thought, without anger. That would come later—after he had time to comprehend the awesome responsibility he had so casually accepted. Spiritual conduit. How could he possibly do that? He had seen Ah Tran after the sessions: spent, wasted, barely able to speak, uncertain of his own identity. They expected him to do this?

He glanced at the clock in the wall. He had forty-two minutes in which to answer his own questions. He sat, struggling with them, but he did not think he would ever get very far.

While he thought, time passed—rapidly.

sixteen

As soon as Ah Tran stepped into the entrance room of his sumptuous quarters, a flock of puzzled servants rushed forward in mass. At least, unlike the android, they appeared to recognize their master even without his usual make-up. He waved the lot of them back and hurried forward. He passed through a large, plush, well-furnished room, then into a smaller bedroom, a large bath, and at last came to a cramped, undecorated, unfurnished room. The ceiling was a wide window open to the star-spangled sky. There wasn't time to give it more than a glance. He carefully sealed the door behind him, then crossed to the far wall of the room. A phone rested here, embedded in the wood. He punched a hasty series of numbers and waited for the viewscreen to glow in response.

When it did, it revealed a heavily painted young woman. She frowned at him quizzically and said, mumbling, "San Francisco Police Department, Felony Division, yes, sir, do you wish to speak to somebody?"

"Inspector Cargill, please," Ah Tran said.

"And who should I tell him is calling?"

He started to tell her, then paused, smiling to himself. If he said *Ah Tran,* he would only succeed in confusing the poor girl; after all, his face was known throughout the world. So he said, "Tell him Donald Tapman."

"Donald who?"

He spelled his last name for her. Twice.

A moment after that, the girl disappeared to be replaced, momentarily, by the impassive visage of Inspector Cargill.

"Now what have you gone and done to yourself?" he asked.

Ah Tran laughed. "Only what you told me to do."

Cargill shook his head. "I didn't say you should do that."

"I know. But I'm afraid I've started taking my responsibilities seriously."

"I warned you that might happen."

"By going to visit the android in his quarters, I assumed the position of an inferior. Since an inferior should never lie to one who occupies a higher position and since all that make-up of mine was really a lie, I decided to take it off. As soon as I'm through talking to you, I'll put it on again."

"Was he surprised?"

"Very."

119

"Did it help?"

"He said yes."

Cargill nodded thoughtfully. He started to smile, then seemed to change his mind: "When?" he asked, after a long pause.

"And who should I tell him is calling?"

"I've scheduled the session in an hour. I assume we don't have much time."

"The war should start sometime tonight."

"Tonight, but—" The news had shaken him deeply. It meant they had no chance at all of succeeding in time. "We've lost."

"Perhaps. They're in a hurry. The primitive nations have received intelligence—from guess who?— describing the inefficiency of the androids. Of course, they feel they have to move now, before the design is corrected."

"Will we be safe here?" Unconsciously, Ah Tran's eyes strayed toward the open, vulnerable ceiling.

Cargill nodded. "Oh, yes. I imagine the fighting will be limited to the usual border zones. It'll turn into an ugly stalemate."

"Which is what they want."

"Yes."

Now it was Ah Tran's turn to pause and consider. He glanced at his watch. "I assume Richmond is doing the designs for the new model."

"Yes, he's supposed to turn them in tomorrow at dawn."

"Do you think he's safe? Surely, they don't want—"

"I doubt it. At this point, they'd kill him in a minute."

"What are you going to do?"

"Go over there and try to stop them."

"Don't leave until you've heard from me."

"I won't—I can't. If they get to him before then—" Cargill gave a sad, philosophical shrug "—then we're in a mess. But there's nobody I can trust to help him— except me. Nobody, I'm beginning to find out, is quite what they seem to be. I can't take that risk. I managed to shuffle Hopkins aside but they still have his wife, you know. I've tried to check her out and, as far as I can determine, she hasn't entered the city but—well, they are supermen."

"Yes." He needed no reminder of that fact. "Are you going to put the question to him?"

"Only if the android fails."

"I think he will."

"Why?"

"Because," Ah Tran said, "I've felt them up there. In that place. Before. It's difficult to explain. It isn't space and yet—in the sense that it can be occupied, inhabited—it is a region that parallels normal space. Our bodies occupy space; our minds, our souls, occupy this other place. Well, I've felt them up there—in there—observing me. When I've taken the gestalt upward. They've never tried to interfere. I haven't come close enough to success for them to make the effort. But, if there was ever any real danger—I'm sure of this—they would act and act at once. The android would never be able to resist them."

"They'd kill him."

"If they could. And I think they could."

"And you too?"

"I hope not," Ah Tran said.

"Richmond might do better."

"I hope so."

"Then call me," Cargill said.

"Will he say yes?"

"He may."

"May?"

"That's the best I can do. We'll be lucky if he's still alive."

"All right," Ah Tran said.

Cargill agreed. "All right."

The screen went blank. Shaking his head slowly, Ah Tran laid down the phone receiver and stepped away from the wall. He glanced briefly at his watch. Forty minutes. He unlocked the door and went into the bathroom and then into the large bedroom. He locked both doors and sat down in front of a dressing table and mirror. He began applying the make-up to his face. He drew wrinkles and creases in the smooth flesh of his face. He turned the bald peak of his skull forty years older. He laid bags under both eyes and dyed his light beard dull gray. He added pockets of sagging flesh to his throat, extended the lobes of his ears, and put a tired twist into the tip of his nose. Then, moving down, he began to roughen the tight skin on the back of his hands.

He knew this other face——the one which, in stages, began to appear in the mirror—far better than he knew his own. But the fact remained: he wasn't Ah Tran; he was Donald Tapman. He didn't feel this made him a fake. He was an actor. Five years ago, he had belonged to a small, communal theatrical company touring the primitive East—Pakistan, Bangladesh, India, in particular. The company performed in native villages—Shakespeare, for the most part—then passed the hat. Poetry for the masses, so to speak. He had fallen in love with the East. Like any intelligent young man born in Brooklyn, he thought it was a very mysterious place. He particularly liked their religions. He had been raised a Baptist. He spoke to gurus, various messiahs, prophets, healers, mystics. Often, because of the extreme poverty in the villages they visited, the company went hungry. He noticed that few mystics—except on purpose—ever went hungry. He learned that, in past centuries, Eastern religions had swept the West briefly in fads. Buddhism would be as popular for a time with Western European intellectuals as cake with the masses. *The Tibetan Book of the Dead*—or the *I Ching*—would top student bestseller lists. Gurus would tour America, reaping material rewards. This did not mean the mystics were fakes; he was sure most—if not all—had been benevolently motivated. So was he. One night, he slipped away from the company, carrying several jars of make-up. Two days later, he appeared in the Western colony of Calcutta. Nobody would have been likely to recognize him. He said his name was Ah Tran and he came from Tibet. (Sometimes he forgot and said Nepal instead.) The new name was meaningless, but he liked the sound the two syllables made together.

Within a week, he had established a small but devoted following. At first, he begged from tourists but, within a month, he had developed and unveiled the philosophy of the circle, the cycle. Further converts quickly came and he required each to sign his worldly goods over to the new messiah. He incorporated the movement, hired a lawyer, built a school of disciples, and left India to tour the world. He never went hungry any more.

And—when?—sometime—three years ago maybe— he had accidentally stumbled across a certain fact of existence which had, at first, nearly forced him to renounce his following and flee for his sanity. By accident—he could not accept the idea of divine intervention—he had discovered what no one except a few mystics had guessed before: that the human mind, under certain conditions, possessed the ability to escape the confines of its body and roam about in a nonspatial place which might well be heaven.

For another year, he had kept his knowledge secret. He ceased meditating; he concentrated on preaching.

Then, last year, Cargill had come to him and exposed the existence of a small group of supermen—the Inheritors. He had thought at first that Cargill, despite his credentials, was merely another crackpot. He had known many such—they were an occupational hazard. But Cargill happened to be telling the truth. The Inheritors did exist. He soon learned this.

Cargill asked for his help. What else could he say? He said yes.

And now here he was. Dabbling his face with a last-minute coat of make-up. Ignoring, as befitted his stature, the insistent rapping on the bedroom door. Five minutes. He was about to risk his life, his sanity and—who knows?—perhaps his soul.

Why? For what?

Why, to save the world of course. What else?

Brooklyn was a long way away.

seventeen

Alec thought this ought to be the only way to live. It was late—past midnight—and he was alone in the rear room of the office seated in front of his desk. In one hand he held a pencil; the other rested upon the top corner of a small notepad. The paper was almost blank—a few vague squiggles. But he was working— yes—thinking, dreaming, calculating, devising, designing, conjuring, and as far as he was concerned nothing at all might exist beyond the boundaries of this one small room. And he liked it that way.

The general had visited him yesterday afternoon. It wasn't Hopkins, with whom he had always dealt before, but another man—American Air Force. General Hopkins, the new man had said, was temporarily on leave. Alec didn't question this assertion—on leave with full-scale war about to erupt at any moment?— because he had long since grown accustomed to the military and its crazy ways.

"We seem to have a dreadful problem," the new general said.

"Well, what?" Alec asked.

"About your androids."

"Well, tell me—it can't be that bad."

"Oh, it is. It's worse. It's awful."

"Tell me."

It seemed—the general related—that during recent field maneuvers, an apparent flaw in the design of the latest model android soldiers had come to light. They—the soldiers—no longer appeared able to hold on to their weapons properly. They could aim well enough—that was not the problem—and even fire a clean initial shot. After firing, they took immediate cover. All of this was fine. But, standing to advance after taking cover, nine times out of ten they forgot and left their weapons behind. Why?

Alec had no compunctions about telling the general

why. It wasn't the design, he insisted. The fault was theirs—the government, the army—in failing to realize that an android was a good deal more than a complicated hunk of machinery. In the last year more than half-a-million had been produced; forty percent of that total had come in the past sixty days. Computers—and all android production was, of course, computerized now—could perform a given task faster and, in most respects, better than any number of human workmen. Computers were fine for producing clocks, tele-visaphones, clothes-making machines, hovercraft, walkway components. But, as far as androids were concerned, an essential factor was missing—the personal factor—the human. The first androids had each been skillfully produced by human hands. The most recent had not. The first androids had been men in almost every sense except birth; the most recent were hardly more than flesh-colored automata. They could move—oh, yes—and walk, talk, aim, fire, fall. But they could not think. They did not seem to be aware that they were supposed to. If the general wanted to build a perfect android specimen, then Alec could tell him exactly how. For each one—each and every android—assign one man to oversee all aspects of that android's production. Let computers push the buttons and read the gauges and operate the conveyor belts. But if the general wanted success, then he needed that one man on the spot.

The general had flushed—almost as if he were embarrassed. "You talk almost like an android needs a mother."

"Yes—or a father. Someone, anyone who is human."

"It's impossible—we don't have the men—or the time."

"It takes a woman nine months to produce a child. An android is no less complicated."

"Impossible."

So Alec had agreed to a compromise. For a flat fee of a million new dollars, he consented to design an android equipped with a modern beam rifle inside its right arm. That way, to fire, the android would only

125

have to point a finger at the target and press down with its thumb on a button implanted in the palm.

"That ought to work," the general had agreed. "Unless they start losing their hands."

"I told you how to solve your problem," Alec had said.

"Impossible—but we'll need this new design right away."

"I'll get right to it."

When Alec told Sylvia Mencken about the new contract, she flew into a furious rage and said she wouldn't sign. He tried to explain—as patiently as he could—that if they refused to sign the government could easily find someone else. The military owned the patents to the original designs and what they now wanted was only a minor modification. Anyone with a smattering of engineering ability could do it. Sylvia calmed down. She explained she had lost her temper because she was sick and tired of the work. She wanted them to have a chance to get away from the city for a few days—maybe even two weeks or a full month—a vacation—go somewhere where there weren't any soldiers or androids or beam guns.

Alec smiled and shook his head. "I don't think there is anyplace like that in the world any more."

"Well, we could try to find it."

"Well, we will. I promised the general I'd deliver the new design by dawn the day after tomorrow. After that, we can go, if the war doesn't catch us first."

"We'll run fast."

He had laughed.

And that was why he was here now—at one o'clock in the morning—doing what he was doing.

Somebody knocked at the door behind.

"Come in," Alec said, without turning around. He knew it had to be Sylvia. She had been in and out all night.

As soon as he heard the beat of her high heels clicking across the floor, he swiveled in his chair.

"Any progress?" she asked.

"Some."

"How much?"

He grinned and answered slowly. "I should be done in an hour or less. All I have to do is write it up."

Oddly, he thought he sensed a flash of radiated disappointment, but then her intense joy and pleasure smothered that. She clapped her hands together and said, "Oh, I'm glad."

"Me too. Now we can get out of here."

"Yes," she said, holding up her hands suddenly. He flinched backward but all it was was a shiny aluminum flask. "Coffee?"

"Sure—anything," he said.

"This is all we have." She leaned over, pouring coffee into his cup. Then she stood up, smiled quickly, and started to go out. Her radiated joy had barely been diminished.

"Wait," he said. She stopped, not turning. "I guess I might as well see him now."

"Are you sure?" She seemed concerned, fearful. "Why don't you just go out and tell him to get lost? I've tried but he just smiles and says it's official business. At one in the morning."

"I suppose he knows what he's doing. But I think I'd better see him." He sipped his coffee, ignoring as best he could the foul, bitter taste. Anna had always made real coffee—she had the beans imported directly from Colombia—and any artificial blend tasted like stagnant water in comparison. "I'll get rid of him as soon as I can, then finish the last of the project, call the army, and go home."

Sylvia opened her mouth as if to speak, then seemed to think better of it. She turned and went out.

Alec swiveled back to his desk.

A few minutes later, the door opened once more and Sylvia came in followed by Inspector Cargill, who nodded vaguely at Alec, then stood in the middle of the room, rocking on the balls of his feet, blowing gently upon a steaming cup of coffee. When Sylvia left, he came over and leaned against Alec's desk. He was wearing a huge, heavy overcoat which concealed his body and shape like a thick winter hide.

"Quite a place you have here," he said, ambiguously.

"What do you mean by that?" Alec asked, leaning back in his chair, glaring up at Cargill.

"Oh, you know. From the front, this could be almost anything: lawyer's office, doctor, even a cop. But, back here—well, you can see—it's the place where a serious man works."

"I also have a laboratory I use."

"I am aware of that," Cargill said, defensively, as if his professional ability had been questioned.

"I thought you would be," Alec said, sighing. What did Cargill want? Were they going to have to sit like this for hours before the inspector got around to exposing his hand? There were times when Cargill never seemed to reach the subject, when he sat for long minutes, talking aimlessly, asking an occasional, usually senseless question, then suddenly standing up, bowing, smiling, leaving. Since the murder of Ted Mencken, Alec guessed he had been visited by Cargill an average of twice a month. He had no clear idea why. He didn't think Cargill suspected him of the murder any longer—if he ever had; it should have been plain enough by now that Alec was innocent. Cargill himself had never changed. His mind remained as taut and controlled as ever. He made Alec no less uncomfortable than the first time they had met. And there was still the matter of Timothy Ralston's murder. He was convinced—despite the dying man's denial—that Cargill was somehow involved. Exactly how, he did not, of course, know."

"How is your wife—Anna?" Cargill asked, his eyes peeping over the edge of his high coat collar. He had intercepted Alec's next line of thought. "I haven't seen her lately."

"She left me nearly eight months ago," Alec said. "Don't tell me you didn't know that."

"I saw one of her tape sculptures recently," Cargill went on, oblivious to Alec's interruption. "An older work, I believe. An excellent piece—quite fine—moving—beautiful."

128

"Not *Crime and Punishment?*" Alec asked, sarcastically.

"Oh, no. This was a wholly original composition. But no less remarkable for that. Your wife is an extremely talented woman, Mr. Richmond. My own, as you may know, is dead."

"I didn't know, but I'm sorry."

"But exactly where is your wife now?"

"I told you. She left me."

"But you've seen her more recently than eight months." He removed a pocket notebook from his overcoat and flipped the pages slowly. "Ah—here it is. She was last seen at your house two months ago— somewhat less than that." He slammed the notebook shut and gazed at Alec expectantly.

A wave of guilt consumed Alec. He tried to shrug it off. Why should he feel guilty? He deliberately told Cargill the truth: "Anna and I don't hate each other. We don't see any reason to attempt to ignore each other."

"As you may know, your wife employed me to do a bit of detecting for her. I undertook the mission in all good conscience. However, sometime after beginning the job, she suddenly refused to answer any of my calls. I received a brief note thanking me for my work and expressing a lack of need to see me again. I was, of course, rather puzzled."

"I—I didn't know about any of this," Alec said. So that was why Ralston had seen Anna and Cargill together before the Mencken murder. "What was this job she hired you for?"

Cargill went on, pretending that he had not heard Alec: "So you can see why I'm interested, concerned. Why I'd like to know where she is now."

"She's with friends," Alec said.

"Where?"

"Oh, back East someplace."

"The Atlantic coast?"

"No, not that far. The Middle West someplace. Wyoming, Colorado."

"How did she get there? The tube?"

"No, it's an out of the way place. The tube doesn't go there. I think she flew."

"What flight? What line?"

"Now look," Alec said. He stood, towering over Cargill. "What's any of this to you? There is a thing called privacy. Anna happens to be my wife—not yours."

"I never insinuated otherwise, though of course I would be honored by the privilege. Still, I wonder about people. You understand—my profession."

"Well, wonder about someone else." Alec stepped back, lingered half in the air, finally sat down. Cargill's stately composure perplexed him. The radiations he gave off were as steady and impenetrable as ever. "To tell the truth," he said, "I don't know exactly where she is. I think it's Wyoming but she wouldn't let me have an address. I think she wants to lead her own life—without me."

"And the android?" Cargill asked.

"The android?" Alec laughed, unable to resist the opportunity. "You mean Eathen? Don't you know? He left at the same time Anna did. He's enlisted in the Ah Tran movement. I wonder if I could demand to have him sent back. Like the fugitive slaves before the Civil War. He's property—not a person. In fact, I think he's actually a disciple of Ah Tran."

"Yes," Cargill said, "he is. But—what I want to know about—" he leaned forward, quivering with suppressed anticipation "—is what about you?"

"Me?"

"Are you intending to enlist too?"

"Hardly. My work is science—not crazy mysticism."

"The two are not incompatible." Cargill leaned back, apparently satisfied at having made some private point, and crossed his hands over the waist of his great cot. "Both are devices by which man attempts to comprehend and measure the vast unknown. With science, the technique is firm knowledge gathered through experiment and observation. With mysticism, sheer inspiration is used. The one follows the other. Einstein, for example, merely confirmed what many mystics had been saying for centuries. When the two are combined—"

"They can't be," Alec said, leaping to his feet. He was strangely and greatly irritated by this nonsense. "If you don't mind, Inspector, I'm very busy. I've enjoyed this talk, but some other time, please."

"Oh, of course. Certainly." Cargill nodded sharply once, smiled, stood, brushing at the front of his coat. But he made no effort to leave. "How about you, Alec?" he said, suddenly. "Aren't you curious about your wife's whereabouts?" He shoved his hands in the deep pockets of his coat, burying them both, and began rocking on the balls of his feet. "I could tell you exactly where she is."

Alec stood up too, sensing the approach of a sudden crisis. "How do you know? Are you following her? Isn't that against the law? Isn't that harassment?" All his months of suppressed fury at Cargill began to pour out at once. "Where she is—where anyone is—happens to be none of your business. Anna is a free citizen. She hasn't committed any crime. She didn't kill Ted Mencken."

"Oh, I know that," said Cargill.

"And neither did I."

"I'm sure of that too."

"Then, if you know so much, maybe you can also say who did kill him."

"Yes," said Cargill, "I can say that. I can say who killed Timothy Ralston also."

"You know—no! You can't know that! You—!"

There was a soft tapping at the door. Alec called, "Come in!" then turned back to Cargill. How could he know? If he knew that much, then didn't it mean he must also know everything, and that was impossible. He had to be bluffing. Some trick designed to force a confession.

"I thought you might like more coffee," Sylvia said, holding the flask out toward Cargill.

"Oh, yes." Cargill smiled. "Thank you." He brought his right hand out of his coat pocket. He reached out toward the coffee. In a flash, Alec realized that the hand was clutching a gun. He saw it for only a split second. He didn't think Sylvia saw it at all. Her expression never wavered. Cargill fired. An inch-wide, gaping, black hole opened in the center of Sylvia's forehead. She didn't utter a sound. The coffee flask slipped from her fingers and crashed to the floor, splattering hot liquid in every direction. Scalded, Alec cried out.

Then Sylvia fell over.

Cargill replaced the gun in his pocket. "Well, how about that?" he said, with amazement. "I did it." He let out a loud, solid, satisfied sigh. He shook his fingers proudly at Alec. "A matter of reflexes, I suppose. And quick, quick thinking." He grinned.

Alec wasn't listening. He was staring at Sylvia's still form, unable to raise his eyes from the sight. She was dead—that was it—dead.

From what seemed a great distance, Cargill's words penetrated his brain: "I suppose I do owe you some sort of explanation."

eighteen

Alec found that he could not concentrate upon Cargill's explanation as long as Sylvia Mencken's body was lying on the floor only a few yards away. Cargill suggested they either move the body or themselves.

Alec didn't want to touch her. "Let's go out front," he said.

They settled in the first room. Cargill carefully checked to ensure the door was locked, then sat behind the receptionist's desk. Alec dropped on the couch.

Not for the first time, Alec regretted he no longer had a gun. How could he have been so foolish as to let Astor's men take it and not give it back? He should have known he'd need it again.

"Why?" Alec said, at last.

"To save you," Cargill said. The tone of his voice

was cold, unemotive, almost official. "And to save our people."

"Save?" he asked, hollowly. "How? By killing the one thing that mattered to me?"

Cargill shook his head slowly. "She meant nothing to you. Ask yourself. Did you love her?"

"Yes."

"Why?"

"Because she was important to me."

"She was going to kill you. The same as she killed Mencken and Ralston and maybe many, many others."

Alec did laugh now. "Are you trying to tell me Sylvia was one of the others? That she killed her own father?"

"That's what I'm saying."

"Well—well, you're wrong. For all I know—and it makes sense too—you might be one of them. How do you know about my people? The only ones who know are us—and them."

"Oh, that's common knowledge," Cargill said, blandly.

"Everyone knows?" Alec asked, without particular disbelief. In his present state, he was willing to accept anything he was told—except about Sylvia.

"The men at the highest levels of government do. And me. It really wasn't much of a secret. If there had only been a few of you—no more than a dozen—and if you had chosen to protect your secret zealously, avoiding personal contact except when it was absolutely essential, you might have been able to remain hidden— though, frankly, I doubt it. In our present society, privacy and secrecy are quite extinct. I assume you are aware of the National Computer Data Bank. Each of us—no matter how outwardly insignificant—occupies a personal niche within that network. Our every known move is recorded and filed. If any one person within the system begins to function in ways differing noticeably from the established norm, then his name pops out. When several names have popped out under similar circumstances, an investigation automatically follows—

133

an attempt is made to determine if any relationship exists among these various names.

"In the case of your people, such a relationship was easily uncovered. You see and visit each other much too often. You intermarry. You talk on the public phone lines and exchange information. All of this, of course, ends up on file. And then there is the one common denominator that most obviously binds you all: lack of known parentage. You are all orphans. Plainly, as soon as this information became known, a full-scale investigation was launched. To your credit, it failed to penetrate your deepest secrets. Other common factors were discovered. Your achievements indicated common ability and intelligence—and also a strong tendency toward erratic conduct and eccentric behavior. The suicide rate among you was ten times the national average.

"The investigators—I have scanned their reports—interviewed employers, employees, fellow workers, acquaintances and—when they could be found personal friends. As I said, nothing was revealed. In the final report, you are described as "Quantity X": a tight, secret conspiracy of intelligent orphans. But the purpose of this conspiracy—if any—remained unknown. Obviously, the highest officials were not satisfied. I was asked to look into the matter. I agreed and promptly uncovered the true facts."

"That we were supermen?" Alec shrugged. He barely heard every other word of Cargill's supposed recollection. He was seeing Sylvia's body. The gaping hole in her skull.

"I should be humble about this," Cargill said. "The solution came less from my own endeavors than by accident. Did you know a man—a Superior, I should say—named Blalock?"

"He jumped off the top of the Ferry Tower."

"Yes. And died. But, before taking the final plunge, in a raving fit—my police duties include suicide as well as murder—Blalock spurted out the brief facts of his life. I suspect others—keeping in mind your racial tendency toward flipping out—have heard the same story.

134

There was one significant difference in the response this time. While the others had undoubtedly dismissed the story as the paranoid ravings of a madman, I chose to believe every word Blalock said."

"Good for you."

Cargill nodded. "Thank you. But—the story I got from Blalock—it was naturally somewhat sketchy and disorganized. So I did some additional checking and snooping and, along the way, managed to uncover a second common denominator, one apparently ignored by the computers as unexceptional—the present dwindling birthrate, you know. I refer, of course, to your lack of natural offspring. Not a statistical impossibility—hardly—but, in view of your lack of known parentage, intriguing."

"We're sterile," Alec said, dully. "So what?"

Cargill nodded, smiling. "I know."

"Is there anything you don't know?" Alec asked, more wistful than arrogant. Cargill's knowledge seemed to strip him of whatever identity he had left to himself. His life was public property. He belonged to others—to Cargill, to anyone with a penchant for snooping. It made him sick.

"I delivered my report," Cargill continued. "The facts as I knew them. That you were an apparently advanced form of humanity. Extremely intelligent. Presumably a mutation. At the time I had not confirmed the presence of the telepathic factor and so did not mention it."

"Not telepathy," Alec said.

"Yes, I realized that soon enough. The limitations of the talent, that is. I got to know a few of you rather well. I asked questions here and there. It soon became clear that no one was able to read my mind, that I could conceal what I wished from you with no great expense of effort and that concealment in itself was not sufficiently extraordinary to arouse suspicion."

"Incomplete," Alec murmured. "Incomplete supermen."

"Well put. Yes—exactly. But—back to my report—I made a recommendation which, as far as I know, was

135

accepted. I described you as a sterile mutation unable to survive into a second generation. Thus, I recommended that no specific action be taken against you. I pointed out that the majority of your people were more apt to aid the common public good through your undeniable ability and intelligence—your android project is a prime example of what I meant—rather than harm it."

"Us?" Alec was laughing. "Harmless? Oh, if only you knew." The revelation that Cargill did not know everything struck Alec as tremendously amusing. He couldn't stop laughing. It was so funny. Then why not tell him everything? Let him know just how ridiculous he was? Harmless? "Don't you read the headlines?" he cried. "Don't you know that war is coming? That civilization is about to perish? Harmless? Us? That war happens to be our war. We started it—you'll fight it—and, in the end, we'll win it."

Cargill shook his head and deliberately radiated great sadness. He waved a limp hand toward the back room. "She started it, Alec. Not you."

He had had enough. He came to his feet, waving his arms furiously. "Leave her alone! Haven't you done enough? You killed her. What more—?"

"Sit down," Cargill said, sharply.

"But—" Alec shrugged and sat.

"Listen to me," Cargill said. "Don't you want to know the truth?"

"Not if it's really all lies. She never started anything in her life."

"Not by herself, no. I'm talking about those men and women—those individuals—Sylvia was one, but hardly the only one—of whose existence you have long been aware."

"The others."

"You call them that. More accurately, they are the unknown mothers and fathers of your race."

"Sylvia? My mother?" Alec laughed.

"That is possible, though not, I grant, very likely."

"Nothing that you say is."

136

"Then—" Cargill smiled "—you tell me: who are they?"

"What? The others? Why, I—" Alec stopped, confused. "I'm not sure. We never really knew. People, I guess. People who learned what we were and tried—they used to burn witches."

"Weren't you listening?" Cargill asked, like a stern teacher correcting a lazy pupil "Didn't you hear me describe my report? A decision was made to ignore your people. I can assure you no vigilante group has been formed to do what the government chooses not to do. The others are not human beings, Alec. Think again."

"I don't believe you," he finally said.

Cargill smiled warmly, as if this were the answer he had been seeking. "Of course you don't. Why? Because they wouldn't let you. But that does not change the facts. They are who they are. They possess the ability—in how great a measure I do not know—to control the thoughts and feelings of others. That was why, as soon as Sylvia entered the room, I knew I had to kill her in an instant."

"And you did," Alec said. They were back there again. In that room. The body. The gaping hole. The blood.

"I employed the same ruthlessness she employed when she murdered Mencken and Ralston. No more, no less."

"Sylvia didn't kill Mencken." There was a fact that exploded that theory. Alec struggled to recollect it. "He was her father."

"Oh, no. Like you, Sylvia was an orphan. She entered Mencken's household some two years ago and rather extraordinarily—since she was twenty-four—he adopted her." Then, displaying the first real human emotion since Alec had known him, Cargill stood up, circled the desk, came over, and laid a thin arm across Alec's shoulders. "I'm very sorry. But the facts, alas, are the facts. They cannot be made otherwise."

"Why?" Alec asked.

"Why did she kill him? That's easy enough. The android project. I believe he wished to stop."

"He used to talk about it but—"

"And he was involved in the Ah Tran movement, I believe."

"Yes, but what—?"

Cargill raised his free hand. "We can discuss all that later. For now, I think it's sufficient to point out that Mencken's murder was not without its blessing. The killing brought me into the case. Knowing who you and your wife really were caused me to take an especially active interest in the matter. I did a little snooping—quite a little, in fact. And there was also the fact that, somewhat before the murder, Anna hired me to find her father. However, before I could complete my investigation, she suddenly—I told you this—took me off the case. I became suspicious. I did a little snooping. I found the father and, in the course of that, cracked the whole mess wide open."

"Her father? You found him. But he's dead, the same as mine."

"I expect yours is quite alive too. Anna's father, a creature named Karlton Ford, lives in Wyoming. He is an extremely wealthy individual. This war you are so eager to claim as your own—my research indicates the greater share of the credit should go to Mr. Ford."

Alec shook his head. In spite of himself, he was listening now. But he was confused. Cargill seemed to enjoy establishing a set of wild premises and then, a moment later, casually destroying the framework he had so carefully erected and introducing some wholly new outrageous fact. "I'm afraid you'll have to explain more fully," he said, at last.

Cargill agreed. Drawing away, he paced the room, telling Alec what he knew about the Inheritors, their plans for the war, their talents and abilities and the nature of their hybrid descendants. "I consider it amazing," Cargill said, "that they did not choose to kill all of you at birth. Too difficult, perhaps—or too dangerous—and they may have guessed that you would prove helpful later in furthering their ends."

Alec held himself in check, striving to suppress the desire, the urge, but finally he could not resist.

He laughed.

Cargill stopped pacing and turned, plainly horrified. "Don't you believe me? I have proof—firm proof—evidence. I can—"

"I believe you," Alec said.

"Then why did you laugh?"

"Because there was nothing else I could do. What do you expect from me, Cargill? You come here and murder the woman I thought I loved—even if I can't remember why I thought I loved her—and then you tell me, when her body's still warm, that she's not even a woman: she's some kind of foul monster bent upon conquering and subjugating not only my people but the whole human race too. I said, what do you expect? Do you want me to cry?"

"I thought you might want to help fight them."

"No."

"But we need your help. That's why I came here. To ask you to please—"

"No," Alec repeated, unhesitantly.

"But you haven't heard my proposition." The control Cargill had always exercised over his feelings was completely gone now. Alec received a barrage of brutal, conflicting radiations—but fear was there, and anger too. Cargill crossed the room and laid a hand on Alec's shoulder. "We can't just give up, can we?"

"I don't care what you do." Alec pushed him away. "Just get away from me."

"But—don't you understand?—I had to kill her."

"No, I don't understand." But that was not true. Alec understood. But understanding was not the same as acceptance, and he did not accept. He stood up and moved away into the room, as if seeking some place of hidden refuge.

Cargill followed him. "Are you willing to let the whole world fall to pieces because of your own temporary whims? You know I'm right. Listen to my plan. I admit we can't stop the war—it's too late for that—but we can ensure that the human race will exist afterward. I know these creatures, Alec, these things, and they are as alien to you and me as if they had originated from beyond the Earth itself. Visit my office. Let me show you my files. Ford himself—you wouldn't believe what he has done. Do you remember the Mozambique extinction ten years ago?"

"I don't care," Alec said, uttering each word separately. The Mozambique extinction, the fate of the human race—he did not care. *Sylvia, Sylvia, Sylvia,* he thought, seeing her body again. *No, no, no.* He had to get out of here and think.

"And Anna?" Cargill was saying. "What about her? Ford is her father. She is with him right now. Don't you understand—?"

"Why should I?"

"She's your wife."

"I told you, Cargill—I don't care."

But Cargill continued to chase Alec like a hungry dog in pursuit of a rabbit. "At least listen to my proposition. It's Ah Tran. He can—"

Alec had heard enough. He whirled, facing Cargill eye-to-eye. "If you aren't out of this office," he said, "in twenty seconds, I swear I'll kill you. I'll take that gun out of your coat and ram it straight down your throat. Now—please—go. Just leave me alone."

Cargill started to speak, then simply shook his head. Alec sensed his surrender. He said, "All right."

"Good."

"But I want you to take this." Eagerly, he pressed a thick plastic card into Alec's hand. "It has my home number. If you change your mind, call me there. It may not be too late."

"There's nothing I can do." But Alec accepted the card.

"You won't know that till you've heard me out."

"I'm ready to die."

"And take five billion people with you?" Cargill did not wait for Alec to reply. He went to the door, unlocked it, then stepped out. As he did, for the first time, he permitted Alec a clear view of the inside of his mind. Alec staggered back, grasping his head. Then

Cargill moved into the corridor and slammed the door behind him.

He was gone.

"Damn you," Alec said. His head was aching. He went over to the couch and started to sit but then remembered what the back room still contained.

He couldn't stay here. No.

He would go home. That was the place to be now. Home. Alone. He would go there and wait.

For the end, he thought *I'm going to go home and wait for the end.* The thought amused him. He laughed out loud.

Throwing open the door, he stepped outside.

nineteen

Karlton Ford had had constructed, upon the roof of his Wyoming ranchhouse, a wide sun porch in the shape of a circle. When activated, a silent mechanism drove the porch in a clockwise direction; it made one complete revolution every quarter hour. Ford loved the sun. Normally, he could lie underneath it all day long and never get burned. Right now, he lay on his back near the edge of the porch. He didn't feel the blistering heat. The porch moved, but Ford was unaware of the motion. Nearby, his daughter, Anna Richmond, lay on her back, one leg bent, a hand laid across her forehead to act as a shield to protect her eyes against the fierce solar glare. She wasn't moving a muscle. During the last few days, Ford had been forced to exercise increasingly greater control over Anna. But she was free of any constraints this moment.

Ford found it difficult to ignore the danger presented by her and concentrate upon the task at hand. He was trying to complete a full communicative link with an Inheritor named Hopkins, who lived in San Francisco. Telepathy—especially over any considerable distance—was a chancy means of contact, but since it avoided any possibility of government interception, the

141

Inheritors always tried to resort to it when immediate communication was a necessity. After establishing the initial link—Hopkins had already done that—the next step was to create the basic mood of the communication. Since Hopkins had called, he was the one doing all the transmitting, but receiving was an even more difficult process. That was why Ford had had no choice but to set Anna free. To do this right, it was nearly necessary to shut off the exterior world entirely. The basic mood Hopkins seemed to be trying to get across was one of extreme anxiety, but Ford was unable to pick up the next aspect. He vaguely saw the outline of a face—a young man?—but he could achieve no more certain identification. He strained and strained, trying to see the face more clearly. He could sense nothing beyond himself now. The face grew more clear. Suddenly, all its features seemed to coalesce into a legible whole. Yes, he thought. He laughed at himself. Of course he knew that face—it was Anna's husband—it was Alec Richmond.

Proceed, he signalled Hopkins, indicating success.

While waiting for the next signal to arrive, he opened his eyes hastily and glanced over at Anna. She still hadn't moved. A good sign. He peered into her mind. Not so good. She seemed confused. Her brain darted frantically from thought to thought, subject to subject. There was neither order nor design to her method. An anarchy of thought. Ford did not like that.

Anna knew much, too much. That was the central difficulty. It might not matter any more—the entire thing might be over in a few weeks—but until then Anna presented an awesome danger. If Anna had been anyone else, Ford would have killed her without hesitation. But she was his daughter and he did not want to kill her. A strange defect, he admitted. An almost human queasiness.

Ah—but here was Hopkins. Another message. Ford turned from Anna to concentrate. An android. Not unexpectedly. An android armed with a rifle. Stepping across a scarred battlefield. The android dropped to a knee. Fired. A moment later, it fell face down in the

142

mud. A shell whizzed past, exploding safely behind. The android stood again and marched ahead. But the rifle had been left behind.

The vision faded. *Proceed,* Ford thought, but he was puzzled. What was the point? The failure of the most recent androids to function properly was well known to the Inheritors. It was part of their scheme. The result of this failure would be to even the conflict, to cause a grand stalemate which, in turn, would tempt both sides into building and using nuclear and chemical weapons. And that, of course, was the whole idea.

Anna moved.

Ford instantly snapped the contact with Hopkins and spun around. He turned just in time to see Anna scamper to her feet. Turning desperately, she suddenly found the right direction and rushed toward the edge of the rotating circle. Ford started after her, quickly probing her mind. What he found shocked him. Anna reached the edge of the circle and leaped off to the roof. She tottered momentarily, then caught her balance and ran on toward the edge of the roof. Ford was only a few feet behind. He reached out, stretching his fingers, but could not hold her. He stopped. He used his mind. He caught her at the edge of the roof and clamped down viciously. She stopped with one foot raised in the air. She stood as motionless as any statue. Ford did not lessen his hold. Anna screamed. He tightened his grasp. She collapsed, falling straight down, one arm dangling over the edge of the roof.

Ford let go.

He hurried the remaining distance that separated them and crouched at her side. He held her wrist in his hand. A pulse. Faint. But she was alive. He pried open an eyelid and peered at the white of her eye. He wouldn't enter her mind. She was unconscious but it was a foul mess in there. He touched her forehead. Sizzling hot.

Ford stood up. *Suicide,* he thought, with disgust. No conceivable act seemed more foul to him—so morbidly human. Animals did not kill themselves—neither should supermen. Suicide was an act reserved for those animals granted—or cursed by—a dim flickering of intelligence. Ford glared down at Anna. He could easily kill her now. Any love or loyalty he might have felt for her was gone now. One gentle shove with his foot and she would be gone, toppling gracefully down to the hard earth below. She wanted to die; let her.

He shrugged off his disgust and turned away. He lay down upon the rotating wooden wheel and shut his eyes. Hopkins returned. He didn't intend to bother with Anna any more. If she woke up while the contact was on and jumped, he wouldn't do a thing to stop her. He wouldn't even say goodbye.

Hopkins's next vision was clear. It was a picture of himself, stark naked, without his usual uniform. Ford comprehended the vision immediately. Hopkins had been stripped of his command over the android project.

Ford signalled, *Proceed*.

The next vision was a fantasy—a possibility. It came in bright, deliberately unnatural colors. Richmond again. In an office—his office. Sitting at a high desk, papers piled in front of him. The vision zoomed close for a near view of the papers. They were designs—drawings—android soldiers. One had its arm raised, finger outstretched. Fire bursting from the hand. The vision immediately faded. In its place came a single word, blazing like neon light: DANGER.

Ford signalled back: *Situation comprehended—action to be taken—confirmation in one hour.*

Richmond had to be stopped. Ford asked himself: How?

He looked at Anna. She had not moved. He answered his own question. He saw a solution with beautiful clarity. The humans even had a cliche for it: killing two birds with a single stone.

He pressed the button sunk in the floor beside his head.

"Yes, sir?" came McCoy's lilting voice.

"My daughter has suffered an accident. Please come and assist her."

"Anna? Oh, no. She's not—"

"She's alive."

"Is she badly hurt?"

"Why not do as I order and see?"

"Yes, sir. Of course, sir."

While waiting for McCoy to arrive, Ford lay motionlessly, soaking up the last rays of the quickly disappearing sun. Seeing Anna, he experienced a vague regret. For a human, he had liked her. She hadn't been wholly stupid. But a necessity, he reminded himself, was just that: it was necessary.

McCoy appeared, dashing hastily across the roof. When he saw Anna, he came to a sudden halt and threw one hand across his mouth. He cried out, slightly muffled, "Oh, no!"

"She'll survive," Ford said.

"But what—what happened?" McCoy rushed to the girl's side.

"It doesn't matter. Carry her down to her room. Leave her there." Ford shut his eyes against the sun.

"Did she fall?"

"I told you what to do."

"Yes, sir," McCoy said. Reaching down, he lifted Anna in his arms and, plainly straining, turned back toward the elevator. He swayed as he walked.

"I'll be down shortly," Ford said. "I want you to remain with her. If she starts to wake, call me immediately. Understand?"

"Don't you think—" McCoy's voice reflected the strain under which he moved "—I should call a doctor?"

"No," Ford said. "I don't."

"But—"

"Do as I say, McCoy."

"Yes, sir."

When he was alone, Ford permitted himself the luxury of laughing aloud. It was the simplicity of his inspiration that pleased him most. Not merely two birds but three would fall from a single stone. Alec, Anna, and the new android. And Anna herself would serve a dual capacity—she would not only be a bird, she would also be the stone.

He established a link with Hopkins and quickly

145

communicated a basic mood of joyful stress. Then he transmitted a fantasy—a possibility. Alec Richmond at his desk, working. Abruptly, from behind, a figure appeared: Anna. She raised a gun and fired. Richmond fell over, dead. Stepping forward, Anna approached the desk and raised the gun, turning the beam to high. She fired at the desk, turning all of Richmond's careful work to ash.

He let the vision fade. What would happen next? Arrest? Suicide? Madness? He realized he didn't care. After her task was complete, he would set Anna free. As a murderer, she would present no danger to them.

Shortly, he received Hopkins's pleased confirmation, with a note of the need for haste.

So he buzzed McCoy: "How is she?"

"Sleeping sir. She seems to be all right. I listened to her heart and—"

"I'll be down in a moment, McCoy. Stay there until I arrive."

"Of course, sir."

Ford entered his daughter's room to find her sleeping soundly. McCoy held her hand between both of his.

As soon as he saw Ford, McCoy dropped the hand as though it had suddenly turned hot.

"Get out of here," Ford said.

"But, sir, I—"

"Out."

"Are you sure you won't be needing me, sir?"

"If I do, I can find you."

"I you want, I could wait outside the door until—"

"No. Find something—anything—and make yourself busy."

"Yes, sir," McCoy said, stiffly.

Ford smiled at the note of anger McCoy left in his wake. But then he turned quickly to his daughter, realizing there was no time for delay. He entered her mind with practiced ease and inserted the necessary directives quickly and carefully. Then he moved back out.

He left Anna on the bed and went out to find McCoy, who was waiting just outside the door. Ford told him to

146

have a plane prepared and programmed for the downtown San Francisco terminal. "Anna wants to go home."

"But isn't she unwell?"

"Do as you're told. When the place is ready, wake
her up. Make sure she leaves. I'll be on the roof."

"But—"

Ford did not feel like arguing. It was already dark.
He left McCoy in mid-sentence and took the elevator
to the sun porch. He didn't need daylight in order to
relax. But he couldn't get Anna out of his mind. She
had so much wanted to find her father. Then she had.
And what was the end result of all her efforts: death
and murder—nothing.

Poor Anna.

But then he realized how fortunate she had also
been. Alone among the self-proclaimed Superiors, she
had been permitted to meet and know her own father.
The fact that this knowledge had brought her great suffering was irrelevant beside the simple truth of experience.

In many ways, Ford thought, Anna Richmond had
been a very fortunate individual.

He smiled and, after that, mourned no more.

twenty

Anna was fighting and fighting and fighting.

But she barely realized what she was doing.

All she knew for certain was that she did not want
to move—that any action at this time would have the
most dreadful consequences—what?—that she was
safe only when she was sitting in one place, doing
nothing.

Programmed in advance, the plane carried her
through the sky without the need for human assistance.
Within an hour after leaving Wyoming, the plane
landed at the central downtown terminal in San Francisco. Anna disembarked at once. She rushed across

the landing strip, raced into the adjoining cafeteria, and bought a mug of coffee. More deliberately, she took a table and tried to control the urge to swallow down the coffee in great burning gulps. She finished the first mug and stood up. She ordered another. Again, she sat, drinking. *Slower*, she thought to herself. *Please—not so fast—slower*.

She drummed her fingers on the tabletop.

Suddenly, a man appeared at her elbow. A stranger. He was sixty or sixty-five with gray hair, gray eyes, and bushy gray brows. He asked:

"Do you mind if I join you?"

"No," she said. "Please—please do."

The man nodded and sat down. His head continued to jerk. He smiled at Anna and said, "Daley. Arthur T. Daley. From the look of me, you wouldn't believe it. Right?"

She said, "No," and tried to probe his mind. But then she remembered that she couldn't do that any more.

"And I bet you can't guess what I am?"

"No," she admitted. "I can't."

He gave a sharp nod. "I'm a mechanic. Believe that. One of the best in the world. There are only a few like me left, don't you know. Work is scarce. But a few people—the very rich—they still like to see a pair of flesh-and-blood hands poking around their cars and planes and boats and gadgets. My son went to college. He wasn't going to be—(the man sobbed aloud)—a mechanic, a bum."

"Is it something to do with your son?" Anna was struggling not to finish the coffee. She wanted this man to keep on talking forever. Her eyes kept darting—without conscious volition—to the clock.

"It's him," the man said. He spoke in very loud tones, as if he could not trust a milder voice to convey his message. Everyone else in the room—it was quite crowded—was aware of his presence. Anna scratched her head viciously, as if the itch she felt emanated from beneath the scalp rather than on top.

Hastily, she asked, "What do you mean?"

148

"The army. They got him. My boy. Do you have any idea how that makes a person feel? On my way home tonight, I looked at the headlines. I don't usually pay much attention to the news, so I didn't know. I mean, yes, I'd heard, but you're always hearing about trouble in the world. This time, though, it's for real. They're going to fight. They're going to try to kill my son."

"Perhaps," she said.

The man did not seem to hear her. "So that's why I went and got like this. I don't care what I do now. This could be the last night of the world. A man has to do something."

"I know."

"It's all been known beforehand. Have you ever read the Bible? The Book of the Apocalypse? This is it. It was written down beforehand."

"I don't believe in that," she said.

"Oh, but you should." The man shook his head pityingly. Anna couldn't remember his name. He gave her a deep, searching look. "A person has to believe in something. If you don't, what have you got to live for? We all need help: you and me, my boy." He waved a hand, indicating the inclusion of the rest of the world. "Who's going to give it?"

Anna started to be honest and shake her head no but then she remembered. Yes. "There is a man," she said, softly. "A person, I mean."

The man shook his head. "There can't be."

"Yes—I know him. I tell you, I do."

"You're lying!" The man reached over and clamped his hand viciously down on hers. "Tell me you are!"

She shook her head. "He is my husband." Her voice was barely more than a whisper. "Alec Richmond."

"I've never—"

Her feet kept trying to move toward the door. In her mind, she kept seeing a sign, which said:

THEODORE MENCKEN
Agent

She had to find it—now!

She sprang to her feet and stood frozen for a moment, her head turning frantically, searching for an exit. Then she saw the door and, ignoring the man's heated protests, turned and ran. But he wasn't about to let her go. He came rushing after her. The eyes of everyone else swiveled to follow their progress.

He caught her at the door.

Holding her elbow, he shouted: "Tell me! How can he help us?" His eyes filled with tears. "Please."

"Androids," she said. "Don't you know? They're going to do all the fighting for us. Your son—he won't have to die."

"I know that," he said, bitterly disappointed.

"You do?"

"It was on the news. Everyone knows that. So what? They'll kill all the androids—and then it'll be my son's turn." He let go of her arm.

So it wasn't true. Alec couldn't help anyone. He was useless—a monster.

She turned and ran outside. The man did not attempt to stop her this time. He was weeping into his hands.

A public walkway ran past the front steps of the terminal. Anna leaped aboard. In spite of the lateness of the hour, the walkway was jammed. She tried to find herself. Where was she heading? People of all types and kinds blocked her view. Not just the usual midnight downtown scum—respectable people too. Well-dressed. As many women as men. Small children. No one seemed to be talking. At least, Anna could hear nothing. She noticed a high building and thought she recognized it. Another high tower. A billboard. The nightly headlines streamed here. In spite of herself, she read the words: "WAR . . . MOBILIZATION . . . WARNING . . . THREAT . . . ANDROIDS . . . ATTACK . . ."

Everyone knew. Alec couldn't help anyone. What had caused her to think he could?

In her mind, a single image dominated. A long dim

corridor. A motionless walkway. Then a door. A sign. The words:

THEODORE MENCKEN
Agent

Again and again, as the walkway carried her into the night, she saw this sign. There was no way she could block it out. Nothing else seemed to matter. The words, over and over, were driving her mad. Suddenly, she realized that this was what had been bothering her all night. The itching inside her skull. She had to find that sign. When she saw it—really saw it with her own eyes—when she passed beyond it—then she could relax; she would be set free.

With a start, she realized she was riding in the wrong direction. She cried out, attracting stares. The walkway was carrying her along the edge of the waterfront, down toward the Marina, away from the towering downtown skyscrapers. The sign was back the other way. She had to find it.

She was maneuvering desperately, trying to find a means of escape, when she saw a cloverleaf ahead. She moved through it carefully, following the signs, and when she emerged from the scramble, she was turned in the right direction. She laughed at her victory. Any moment now. She bit her hand to keep from screaming.

Someone beside her reached out and grabbed her hand.

She turned to look. A young man—good-looking in a well-scrubbed way. But she didn't know him.

"Is something wrong?" he asked, leaning close in spite of the silence around them. He pointed at her fist between her teeth. "I thought—"

She removed the hand and said, quickly, "Thank you—I'm fine."

"But aren't you Anna Richmond?"

"I am," she said, after a moment's consideration.

His smile glowed. "I've always admired your tapes tremendously." He laughed hollowly. "Isn't it funny I'd

151

meet you tonight—of all nights?" Then, in an entirely different tone: "Tonight must be the worst night ever."

Anna was barely hearing him. She had managed to reach the farthermost lane of the walkway where she could watch the streets and buildings as they passed. She was looking for the right place to exit. She could see the sign as clearly as if it were an inch in front of her face. "What is?" she asked, vaguely.

"I mean this war."

"Why? Don't you want it? Don't you think it's necessary?" For some reason, she thought everyone felt this way.

He laughed and held her arm tightly. "I know you're just testing me. I think the whole thing is crazy. Us and them—it would be so easy to live together."

"Would it?"

"Of course. They hate us because we're rich. We hate them because they hate us and because there are more of them than us. So the solution—I told you it was easy—is to spread the wealth around, share it. If everyone is equal, then no one has any reason to hate."

"But everyone isn't equal," she insisted.

"I meant materially."

"But that's just a symptom. It isn't a cause." Where had she heard these words before? She sensed they were not her own. Oh, yes—Alec. Alec Richmond.

"I think it's worth trying. Anything new is worth trying."

"What's new about it? What about communism? That didn't work."

"Communism was a lie. Anyway, it was based on false premises. Marx. . . ."

She let him run on. Since the words weren't hers, she saw no reason to defend them. His sincerity dazzled her. Suddenly, she heard herself saying—these words were not her own either: "I love it. War. The bombing. Shooting. Fighting. I think war is the perfect metaphor for human life." Maybe she was wrong—maybe these words were hers.

She could tell she had shocked him. But wasn't that

the idea? The one thing she didn't need tonight was an admirer.

"But your tapes," he said. "I've seen them all. You can't feel that way."

"But I do."

"The tapes—"

"I was hungry."

"But you're rich. Your family—"

"A person can be hungry for a lot of things besides food. Admiration. Respect. Status. Maybe I just wanted to prove that I was as human as anyone else."

"But I could tell—I felt that you—"

He was not the right person to tell. Who was? Except Alec? She recognized that building there. Yes. It was the one that contained the sign.

But she did not get off the walkway. Darting ahead, she slipped between bodies, escaped the young man. The walkway carried her away. The building faded behind.

She rode for hours. Once more, she was fighting and fighting and fighting. Again, she was barely aware of what she was doing.

But—at last she couldn't resist. The sign drew her onward. She looked up. The building loomed above her. She had arrived.

She sensed it was too late now for anything but moving ahead. She entered the building. The lobby was dark and empty. She found an elevator, entered, and allowed it to carry her up.

Then it was her dream all over again. She saw the dim corridor. The motionless walkway. She moved ahead. In the pocket of her suit, she felt the slick plastic handle of the gun. It was a beam weapon. She placed her finger around the trigger. It was almost time now. She would knock. He would tell her to come in. And then . . . then. . . .

She turned and faced the door. The sign read:

THEODORE MENCKEN
Agent

The sight—so familiar—made her want to laugh. Raising a fist, she stifled the urge. She removed the gun from her pocket. She pointed the barrel straight at the door. Then she knocked—firmly.

But no one answered.

Gently, she called: "Alec? Can you hear me? Open the door. It's me—it's Anna."

Still, no answer.

She touched the knob. It turned easily and then—unexpectedly—the door popped open. Beyond, a small room was filled with yellow light.

She stepped inside and closed the door.

"Alec?"

Where was he? She searched the first room carefully, then went into the second. Nothing here either. No people.

Once more: "Alec?"

Then she went ahead, opened the last door, peered into the last room. The light was on here too.

She saw the body lying on the floor.

At first she thought it was Alec. She had killed him and then forgotten all about it and come a second time. Wasn't that funny? Or maybe this was a dream. She was being forced to relive the act again and again. This was her punishment. They were never going to let her wake up.

Then, stepping closer to the body, she realized it couldn't be Alec. It was a woman.

She turned the body over and looked at the face.

At first, she didn't know. It wasn't herself. Who was it? Recognition came slowly. She remembered a tall, tall building. An outside elevator made of glass. Eathen.

Oh, oh, oh, yes. Sylvia Mencken. She had a gaping hole in the center of her forehead. And she was dead.

Anna, kneeling beside the body, cradled the unused gun in her lap and rocked on her heels. She began to sing: "Sylvia—poor Sylvia—dead Sylvia—poor, lousy, dead, dead, dead . . ."

She started to laugh.

It wasn't so bad. Hey, her head didn't itch any more.

She had passed the sign and now she was free. Alec was saved. Nobody was going to kill her any more.

She did laugh.

Then, suddenly, her body jerked stiff. She sprang to her feet, balancing on the tips of her toes like a dancer. She threw her hands high in the air. She screamed. She fell over.

On her back, she shook, trembled, twitched. She was fighting and fighting and fighting. He had promised. He had told her. The sign . . . the sign . . . the sign. . . . She had passed it.

Someone was laughing.

It was useless. She fought and fought and fought.

She lost.

Standing, no longer shaking, she reached down carefully and retrieved the beam gun. She placed the weapon gently into her pocket. Then she turned and went obediently toward the door.

She passed into the second room. Then the first.

Within her mind, a single image dominated everything. There was no room for other thoughts; resistance was inconceivable. A big house set high on a hill. Dawn. An eerie orange glow spreading across the surrounding countryside. The house was shaped like a square doughnut. At its center, not a hole—a plush green garden.

She had to go here. She had to enter that garden and then she would be free.

A man stood in the center of the garden. A narrow stream, flowing briefly. A high arched wooden bridge.

"Alec," she whispered. "Alec—I'm coming."

She stepped out into the dim and silent corridor and went to find the elevator.

twenty-one

With the faint first light of dawn streaming across the naked flesh of his back, Alec Richmond sat on a bare strip of grass in his garden and sipped orange juice through a straw. Long ago, Alec had removed the glass dome from over the garden, preferring the natural light and heat of sun and moon and stars to their more demure and artificial replicas. Because of this, many of the more exotic varieties of foliage in the garden were now wilted, dead, or dying. Only the sturdy, experienced, native American varieties had managed painlessly to withstand the casual poisons which lurked within the local atmosphere, remnants for the most part from those ugly years before the human race had been forced to learn—however dimly—that nature could kill men as easily as men could attempt to kill nature.

He had chosen this open space deliberately because it was one of the few places in the garden that did not make him think of Anna. She had always liked trees and bushes, running water and high bridges. There was nothing like that here: just grass, a few decaying plants, maybe a worm or two.

He crossed his legs beneath him and continued to sip. The house was far enough distant so that if the phone in the living room decided to ring he could easily pretend not to hear it. He had already disconnected the garden extensions. He felt good now, clean, able to luxuriate in a degree of privacy he had not known in years and years, if ever.

It was a shame he had promised the general his new android model so soon. It must be well past six o'clock by now. Soon enough—probably before seven—his failure to appear with the promised designs would seem suspicious. They would try to call him—first at the office and finally here at home. By eight, their patience should be exhausted. He set eight-thirty as the likely time for them to reach the office. Before nine, they would reach him here.

But that still gave him three hours alone. And the war might well delay them too. As soon as he stepped through the front door, the tridee screen in the living room—which neither he nor Anna ever watched—had automatically blossomed into life, revealing a dull man who spoke with an unemotive voice. War had been de-

156

clared. Hostilities had commenced. And on and on and on.

Removing the poker from its place on the fireplace hearth, Alec had driven the end straight through the tridee screen, coolly destroying—in a flash of sparks, a buzz of shorted wires—both the man and his voice.

From there, he had gone directly to the garden.

Alone. Three hours. Less now. What to do, what to do? How should he spend these final few hours? Should he simply sit and sulk and mourn for Sylvia? Or should he be more active: sit and curse and spit hatred at Cargill? Or what about Anna? He had barely given her a thought, despite Cargill's warning that she might be in great danger.

How lucky Anna was.

She had been permitted to meet and know her own father. If he happened to be—as Cargill asserted—something ugly and despicable, a monster who would calmly squash her underfoot without a second thought—well, that was really irrelevant; what mattered was that he was still her father.

What about his own?

At the government home, when Alec turned thirteen, the director, Mr. Eliot, had called him in—it was official procedure—and congratulated him on his birthday. Then, reading from what appeared to be—from the rear—an official state document, Mr. Eliot began to discuss Alec's own father. He had been, said Mr. Eliot, a mechanic and for years had worked on his own, repairing broken machinery, tending to the maintenance of cars and planes and other devices and gadgets. All of this was recorded (or so Mr. Eliot claimed) in the official state document. But the need for human mechanics was fast disappearing; machines could fix other machines far more efficiently than any pair of human hands. The profession moved toward obsolescence—it would soon be as unnecessary as ditchdiggers, bootleggers, or Indian scouts. So Alec's father had been forced to move farther and farther away from his real enemy—civilization. Eventually, in a cold corner of Alaska, he had met and married Alec's mother, who had soon died while giving birth under very primitive conditions to Alec. But, even here, work was scarce. Soon, there was not nearly enough to support a man and his son. Alec's father had been faced with a decision: he must choose between his work and his son. He could remain where he was—in the civilized world—and risk starvation. Or he could emigrate—to any primitive nation—and find his services well-required and his belly quite full. He would not be permitted, of course, to take his child with him if he left the civilized world; the law required the boy to enter a home.

"But," Alec had asked Mr. Eliot, unable to restrain himself despite the fear he felt for this man, "why didn't he retrain? Wouldn't they let him?"

They would but—he saw no other alternative—Mr. Eliot would cover this point quite bluntly. The fact was that Alec's father had refused retraining. The only open professions at that time—and the situation was little different today—were artistic and electronic. Alec's father had no interest in or knowledge of the arts, and he further rejected official denials that any such interest or knowledge was necessary. No. And, as far as electronics was concerned, he flatly refused that too. He didn't mind fixing machines—he loved the work in fact—but he wouldn't work any closer with them. It was a point of personal pride. In any man-machine relationship, Alec's father believed, one party must dominate—and he felt it had to be and ought to be—the man. Perhaps this view was obsolete. He didn't know. But it was his view, and it meant enough to him that he was willing to sacrifice his son and leave his homeland forever.

"Where did he go?" Alec asked, boldly.

"Africa," said Mr. Eliot, peering over the edge of the official document. "Senegal. But—I warn you—don't try looking for him when you leave this home. You will be sorry—very sorry. You won't find him. He won't be there."

Alec had accepted this advice. For some reason he

had known as soon as Mr. Eliot spoke that it was true. Anna had acted otherwise.

And she had been the one to win.

After that, Mr. Eliot had shown him the tridee photograph. A middle-aged man—but tall, strong, smiling. A black beard. Blue shirt and blue jeans. "This is your father," Mr. Eliot had explained, "the way he looked the day he left you with us. Don't expect him to be that way now."

"Yes, sir," Alec had said.

And was he? In other words, which picture was true? The one shown him by Mr. Eliot—or the other, the Cargill version? Man or monster? Mechanic or superman? Callous killer or loving father?

Or both?

Alec crossed the open grass and crouched beside a budding flower. Was it any different from this? Bending way down, he placed his nose close to the tiny red blossom and he sniffed.

There were two worlds. In one, this flower was a collection of molecules, capable of being broken down into its component particles. More importantly, it could be explained. The fragrance, the shape, the color—all of this could be explained. But in the other world—a place where things existed in the form they ought to possess—this same flower was only an object of rare and unique beauty, a divine creation of color and scent, form and structure and feeling. Two worlds— and they could not be merged. One must accept either one or the other. The world of science—the world of poetry. The way things were—or the way things ought to be. In the past, Alec had tried to combine the two. He had created life through science, but the thing which had emerged in the end (the android soldiers) had been all science and no life—no poetry. Or take Ah Tran—the new messiah—another presumptuous advocate of fusion: the poetry of compassionate mysticism and the science of natural ecology. It wouldn't work. It could not be done. One or the other—never both.

Bending down, Alec plucked the flower and held it

lightly between his fingers. He made his choice: poetry. He did not want a world where things could be explained. He wanted a place where everything—flowers, androids, gods, fathers—existed in the form they ought rightly to possess.

Anna's failure to know and decide had driven her mad. That was her own fault, but his too. When he first met her, he now recalled how impressed he had been—glancing into her mind—by the depth of knowledge and wisdom she possessed. To have these qualities close at hand on a more or less permanent basis, he had married her.

Well, that was another mistake—a failure to choose. Love, marriage, romance—the stuff of poetry—undertaken for reasons of curiosity and study—science again. The marriage had failed. What else?

He wished he could see her now. Anna. If nothing else, he could at least explain the truth to her. None of them had given him the time. From every conceivable side, they had hemmed him in. Astor, the Inner Circle, Cargill, Sylvia, Anna, General Hopkins. If only they had allowed him to think—he would have seen the truth before it was too late.

They would, of course, be coming soon. He would not be permitted to remain free for long but, if nothing else, he had found the time to see the truth and that was something they would never be able to take away from him.

An enormous bang cracked the silent sky. He laughed. Sonic boom. Rocketplane. War.

If nothing else, the generals and admirals—wittingly or not—had finally seen the truth. In the past, they had tried to make of war a thing of fusion—another hybrid of science and poetry. On the one hand, the genuine glory of battle—the expressions of daring and real courage—love and self-sacrifice—patriotism and ideals —the poetry of both victory and defeat. On the other hand were creations of science: the weapons that grew progressively more powerful—from sticks and stones to hydrogen bombs. Science came to supersede poetry. Men were no longer necessary in order to wage a war. And now, at last, android soldiers. There would be no glory in this new war—no courage or love or self-sacrifice. It was science's war—quick, clean, efficient. And meaningless.

Enough. Alec stood up. His thoughts had come full circle. They would be coming soon enough and, when they did, he would simply tell them: *I am through.* No more vain attempts to merge what did not belong together. No more android soldiers. Let them accuse him of murdering Sylvia—he had no idea what Cargill intended to tell them—and he would not demur. A cell. Quiet. Tranquil. Not just prisoners but monks—mystics—often lived in cells. Peace. The perfect domain for someone who now fully accepted the existence of a world where things existed only in their most perfect and inexplicable states.

He had made up his mind. He turned toward the house. As soon as he did, he saw her. She came close to him. Raising a tentative hand in welcome, he said:

"Anna."

Then she fired.

A beam gun!

He cried out. The first burst exploded at his feet, digging a hole a meter deep in the soft ground. He looked down at this gaping pit, unable to comprehend the fact of murder, then lifted his gaze and met her eyes. The gun was clenched in her fist.

He stepped forward. "Anna, no, I—"

He saw her finger tighten around the trigger. Her face and eyes—her lips—were expressionless.

She fired again.

If he hadn't fallen aside at the last possible moment, the beam would have cut him in half. Instead, it struck the thick trunk of a tree behind him. The tree toppled neatly over backward and burst into flames.

"Anna!" he cried, looking up at her. He crawled forward. If only he could tell her—force her to understand. "Please—I must—I—"

Once more, she fired.

The beam dug a furrow through the earth, cutting as straight as a plow, barely brushing the extended fingertips of his left hand. Flowers, shrubs, bushes, small trees blazed with fire. He screamed and shook his left hand. There was no real pain. He looked at the fingers: the tips were gone, neatly and cleanly amputated.

He screamed and staggered to his feet. "I'm hit!" The next burst of fire was inches away. He stared at the pit and then, holding his wounded hand in his good fist, turned and ran back toward the garden. He went only a few yards. A wall of fire stopped him. The flames leaped high into the air. There had to be a way around but—

He turned and faced his wife. "No!"

She came toward him. The flames beat at his bare back, but he could not move. Anna held the gun steadily in front of her. He was screaming, shaking his arms, showing her his wound, but unable to express the truth he knew so clearly.

She was three yards away. Two. He fell silent, not moving, studying her feet. Her mind was dead. She radiated nothing. What was she? An automaton? An android? A product of pure science—devoid of thought, feeling, love? His wife? Anna?

Alec closed his eyes, waiting for the end.

But it never came.

He fainted.

Time must have passed. He was lying on the ground. He felt the fire on his bare flesh. He opened his eyes and peeked but Anna wasn't anywhere.

Instead, it was Cargill who crouched beside him. Cargill shouted: "Hurry! The fire! We've got to get out of here!"

Alec could see the flames darting through the tops of the trees, spreading toward the house. The air was filled with smoke. He could barely breathe. Cargill helped him to his feet. Together, they ran toward the house.

It wasn't until he reached the living room—dense with smoke—that Alec refused to go any farther.

"Anna!" he cried, gesturing toward the garden. "She was there! She was—" He started to turn back.

Cargill reached out and grabbed him. "Anna's dead." He tugged at Alec's sleeve.

"No!" Alec shook away. "I didn't see her! She must be—!"

"She's dead!" Cargill cried. The fire had reached the roof now. Suddenly, part of the ceiling collapsed, spraying them both with plaster. Ghostlike, Cargill stuck out a pale hand and grabbed Alec by the shoulder: "Hurry!" he cried.

This time, Alec did not resist. Together, they stumbled toward the door. Cargill kicked it open. They went out. Coughing, weaving, they went down the winding pathway. Neither stopped until they had passed out of direct sight of the house.

Then Alec fell to the ground and lay there, gasping and heaving. A cloud of smoke rose into the air, forming thick black clouds.

Alec reached up and touched the top of his head. Something hurt. He felt a smooth round bump—and blood.

He looked at Cargill, who was sitting calmly in the grass, as if nothing had happened. When Cargill did not speak, Alec began to swear at him.

"You did it!" he cried. "You killed her!"

twenty-two

As soon as the android appeared, the circle formed quickly around him. Twenty five men and women in a small, white, bare room. Ah Tran sat with his legs crossed underneath him, no different from the other two dozen. He placed himself demurely between two lumpy, plainfaced young women. Recent converts. Sisters. Father as rich as Midas. He bowed his head. He focused his gaze on the floor. His expression was determinedly blank.

The android stood alone in the center of the circle. Tall—though not exceptionally. Palefaced. Wiry black hair. The android was the sort of person, physically, who might result if all the world's population were mixed in one big vat and from this brew a typical man were created. The android was that man. Typical—average—common. Ah Tran despised his very existence here.

But, right this moment, the android—Eathen—Arthur—was the single most important person in the whole world.

Even if he wasn't a person, Ah Tran thought.

He began to mumble. The others hastily joined in. The android sat down, nodding at the others. For the most part, the disciples were rigidly similar: young, white, handsome, slim, respectable. Of the twenty-four, nine were men and the rest were women. All were equally respectable—at least their parents were. And rich too, of course. The disciples had their faces scrubbed clean—their teeth glistened. What they were—Ah Tran had often searched for the one right term before deciding upon this one—they were dilettantes—amateurs. When Ah Tran called, none had seen any reason not to come running at once. Religious feeling was a thing nowadays limited to the rich. Not faith or acceptance or conviction, but real feeling. None of this was to say that the disciples were not in earnest. They were deadly serious—they believed in Ah Tran as the new messiah. Had he told them to kill, he thought they would have acted at once. But that wasn't what he asked. Instead, he asked each of them to do this: to sit in a circle and surrender his identity, to allow that identity to merge with those of the others until a fused whole was created which would then—through a conduit—be sent spiraling upward toward the heavens. He asked them to do this—and each said yes.

It was happening already. Experience and practice made the impossible seem easy. He sensed the gestalt forming around him. He remained deliberately, outside, laboring at the edges of the growing mass, exuding a careful aura of total contentment and serenity, working to weld the temporary fusion of spirits into a secure and final whole which could then be sent forward to take possession of the waiting void of the conduit.

The strain of not acting was immense. At the previous sessions, Ah Tran had always acted as the conduit. As such, he had always ensured that the gestalt was properly fused before allowing it to enter and obliterate his own consciousness. But he had told the android not to try that. He had instructed him to commence his own process of obliteration, to create his own void. The android had done so. Where he sat, there was nothing but the vacant husk of his own body. When he thought in these terms, Ah Tran had to resist the impulse to laugh. Gestalt, conduit, fusion of spirits—it was all the old spiritualist mumbo-jumbo that he thought he had taken over for the simple expedient of getting rich. Well, he was rich, but there was something else besides: the mumbo-jumbo—at least this part of it— happened to work.

So he didn't laugh.

It wasn't telepathy. He didn't believe in that. But he did believe—the evidence forced him to believe—that separate human minds could merge and that these minds, in unison, were far more powerful than any two minds in isolation. There would be twenty-four minds working here. Ah Tran wasn't ignorant. He knew that many past psychologists had theorized the existence of a unified racial consciousness that existed above and apart from individual memory or awareness. So why couldn't—this was his own theory—that racial consciousness be reformed, welded together, and repaired, and then sent upward into the nonspatial domain which was its proper dwelling place? In the Orient, meditation had long been accepted as the proper technique for achieving salvation, so Ah Tran—when he formed his movement—had of course adopted it as an integral part of his new gospel. But the Eastern mystics were wrong. They practiced meditation as a means by which the ego could be momentarily obliterated. What they failed to recognize was that this was only a first step. Ego-death was only another means, it was not an end in itself. Obliterate the ego—yes—but do not stop

165

there, continue on, discover the mass racial wholeness that lies just beyond the next horizon. Ah Tran had done that. Accidentally, it was true. But he had done it and now he knew.

The fusion continued. Ah Tran felt its presence in an almost physical way. It was the mass racial mind of twenty-four—so far twenty-three but he would be joining them shortly—separate individuals.

But it was the third step—the one following meditation and ego-death—which had so far eluded them: transcendence, the passing of the fused gestalt into its higher and proper realm of existence.

Ah Tran looked briefly at the android. What he saw shocked him. The slackness of the android's expression, the ghostly paleness of his flesh, the stillness of his breathing, the absence of tension in his muscles. This man, Ah Tran thought fearfully, though only for a moment, is dead.

But no. The android was not dead. At least, not in any physical sense. He was not even a man—he was a flesh and blood machine—and, as such, was proving, as Ah Tran and Cargill had hoped, to be the perfect conduit. Ego-death would be simple for him: killing a child was always a simpler process than slaying an adult man.

Around the circle, the others were ready too. Ah Tran sensed that it was time. Close. Very close. He could feel them—no, it—waiting for him to come.

But he hesitated. Could the android be expected to bear the strain? In the past Ah Tran had willingly risked his own life and sanity, but now he was demanding that another—an innocent—take these same risks. Did he have that right? His doubts, previously stifled, rose in tremendous unity.

But he had to decide *yes*. Not *yes, he had that right,* but rather *yes, it was necessary.* Outside these peaceful walls, the future existence of the human race was threatened. It sounded like a line from a creaky old melodrama, but if life could sometimes be seen to follow art, why not melodrama too? Besides, the android wasn't human. What God gave, God could take

166

away; what man (as God) gave, he could also take away. Wasn't that logical? Didn't that make strict sense? Ah Tran shut his eyes. He leaned easily back. He made his mind an utter blank. *I am no one. Ah Tran is gone. I am not he. I am no one, not any one, he is dead. . . .*

And when Ah Tran was gone—the spirit which had once been his merged with the fused mass of the gestalt—then the entirety of the twenty-four could finally rush forward to enter and consume the empty vessel which had once been Eathen.

After that—for a moment that seemed to stretch endlessly—utter silence dominated the tiny room. Twenty-five empty bodies sitting motionlessly, as if all life had been drained from them. Nothing moved, breathed, thought, spoke.

Then—at the center of the circle—Eathen screamed.

A moment afterward, he let go a second dreadful cry. The muscles in his arms and legs and chest tightened. He sprang to his feet. He clawed at the top of his skull. He howled. Wailed.

Finally, he fell over. To his knees. Hands clenched in front of his chest. Fingers interwoven. A brief, fleeting expression of horror passed across his face. Then he fell over on his face and, after that, didn't move.

Ah Tran was the first of the circle to awake. Seeing Eathen, he rushed forward and knelt down. He turned Eathen over on his back. Leaning down, Ah Tran seemed to be kissing the android. Actually, he was trying to force the air from his own lungs down Eathen's throat. As he labored, the others also awoke and came forward, gathering in a circle to watch the attempted resurrection. When Ah Tran breathed, Eathen's chest expanded. When Ah Tran backed off to rest, nothing happened.

A minute passed.

Two minutes.

One of the disciples—a young, thin, handsome girl—broke the silence: "He's dead."

"No," said another. "Ah Tran will save him."

"It's been too long," the girl insisted. "I took a class once. His brain is damaged. Even if—"

"He's an android. He doesn't have a brain."

Another, speaking in a voice filled with uncertain awe, said, "Didn't you feel that—that thing up there?"

"I did, yes."

"Me too."

"Yes."

"I think all of us did."

Ah Tran continued to force air down Eathen's throat, into his lungs, heart, bloodstream.

"It was like—I can't explain it. I don't remember." She shook her head.

"I do." This was the first girl—the one who believed that Eathen was dead. She spread two fingers minutely and showed them to the others. "We were this close. To that place. We were floating up."

"We were going to make it," said another.

"I saw the White Light."

"Oh, that's silly superstition."

"I saw something."

"We were going."

"Yes. Oh, yes."

"But then something—I don't know—that—that thing. It stopped us."

"Something lives up there."

"It came down and stopped us. The pain was awful. It was like hurting without being hurt. The pain was all inside."

"And—" the girl pointed at Eathen "—it killed him."

Ah Tran drew away. He leaned back on his haunches and wiped the sweat off his face. He peered down at poor dead Eathen and wondered if death for an android was the same as death for a man. Of course, there was no way of knowing for sure; he had no idea. But he did find it hard to accept that androids might have souls. Wouldn't death for one of them have to have the same insignificance as death for a car or plane—any gadget or machine—not death but merely cessation, a blackness, the end? But Eathen had never

168

been a machine. Ah Tran, who had known him, knew better than that. Eathen had been as close to a man as any creature could possibly come without actually being a man, and maybe that last wasn't true: maybe—by the end—Eathen had indeed become a man. Who could say? Did he have a soul? How was Ah Tran supposed to know that? He was dead—that was all—but the meaning of that death would long remain a veiled mystery.

He stood up.

The girl asked him: "Is he dead?"

Ah Tran said, "Yes."

One of the young men asked, "What was that thing we felt up there? Did you feel it too?"

"I did."

"But you don't know what it was?"

"I know."

"Can we kill it? Or go around it? Does it live up there? Does it mean we'll never make it?"

"I don't know yet."

"Well, tell us what it is," another broke in. "We have a right to know."

"No, you don't," Ah Tran said. He hurried toward the door without another word. Nobody tried to stop him or follow. He went into the room that served as his bedroom, locked both connecting doors, then lay down on the bed. He knew he ought to call Cargill; he should have done it as soon as he woke without wasting time trying to play messiah and bring back to life a man—or android—who was already thoroughly and irrevocably dead.

But he knew what it was that had stopped them up there. He even knew its name.

It was Karlton Ford.

But, still, he did not get up to call.

twenty-three

As soon as the plane safely reached a straight and level course above the clouds, Alec turned in his seat and faced the pilot, who sat hunched behind the wheel, eyes rigidly focused upon the thick glass of the forward windshield. Alec had to tap him gently on the shoulder to attract his attention.

Cargill turned and smiled at Alec.

"I have a right to know what's going on," Alec said.

"Eh?" said Cargill. He cupped his ear and grimaced painfully. "I didn't catch that." He turned back and faced the windshield.

The plane was a classic, battered, twin-engined jet. The noise of the engines thundered through the tiny cramped cockpit.

Alec shouted: "I want to know what happened back there! At the house! If you didn't kill her, who did?"

"Weren't you there?" Cargill was shouting too. "At the house, I mean." He smiled, then shook his head to indicate his confusion. "I was sure you—"

"Now wait a—" Alec began.

Cargill waved him silent. The small viewscreen in the center of the plane's control panel was flashing in a brilliant display of rainbow colors. Cargill reached out and removed the phone. The viewscreen failed to clear. Cargill began to talk, barely whispering. From what little Alec could overhear, they were being ordered to land immediately.

Turning in his seat, Alec looked outside. Beneath lay a soft, plush, unbroken layer of lazy white clouds. They had left the ground flying east but he had no way of knowing where they were going now. North, south, east, west—didn't you always end up at the same place in the end? The Earth, after all, was a globe and that meant—

He turned back. Cargill, apparently involved in a fierce dispute, was waving his arms angrily at he talked. The plane dipped and swayed as his attention wavered. The whole situation was very strange. Here Alec was—up above the clouds—going he didn't know where—and the funny thing was he couldn't ever recall agreeing to come.

He remembered the drive—in an old diesel car—to the air terminal in Berkeley. He remembered Cargill leading him toward the plane. He recollected an angry debate before they had been granted permission to take off. All of that was clear; what wasn't clear was why.

Alec heard a click. Cargill had replaced the phone and was now chuckling softly to himself.

"Now what?" Alec asked, remembering to shout.

But Cargill, when he replied, spoke in a normal conversational tone. It irritated Alec to find he could easily hear every word quite clearly: "A fool. Wanted me to land. Because of the war, they seem to feel they now own the air itself. Fortunately, as was the case in Berkeley, my credentials managed to convince them of my legitimacy."

"In other words, you lied to them."

"Hardly. I merely insisted my business was urgent. Which it certainly is. I merely hope the various bodies we have left scattered around remain undiscovered until we have landed. I would hate to be shot out of the sky."

"Then you better get a parachute," Alec advised. "They're sure to find Sylvia." He explained about the android project and his deadline.

Cargill chuckled again. "Oh, that's no problem. Before speeding to your home, I contacted your general—an acquaintance of mine, incidentally—and informed him you were a traitor."

"That was nice of you."

"I suggested he send a squad of investigators to a certain place in Oregon. I told him that was your suspected hideout. Fortunately, I have visited the area in the past and can vouch for the presence of a cabin there. A refuge, in fact, from certain cares of the world." He smiled in recollection.

"And he believed that story?"

"Of course. Don't you?"

"No, I don't."

"Well, frankly, my integrity has never been questioned before."

"No, but—"

"And I do not care to have it questioned now." Cargill suddenly found something of extreme interest down among the clouds. He leaned over in his seat, staring out his window. Alec looked out too, but could see nothing beyond the unbroken layer of white clouds. As usual, Cargill's thoughts were under stern control and nothing peeped out.

When Alec turned back, Cargill was regarding him with an amused grin.

"About Anna . . ." Alec began.

"Fifteen minutes," Cargill said. He glanced down at the controls. "Twenty at the most."

"I didn't ask—"

"Ah Tran is particularly eager to meet you."

"Who? That crackpot? Look here, is this—"

"Of course it isn't."

"Well—"

"Look," Cargill said, waving at the interior of the plane. "Perhaps I'm wrong. But you are here, aren't you?"

"Not by choice."

"Oh, I see. You're accusing me of kidnapping."

"No, of course not. But you did—"

"Coercion? What kind? Physical? Mental? Spiritual?"

"No, none of that. But I—"

"Then I really don't think—" Cargill assumed a pained, hurt expression "—you ought to imply otherwise."

"But I didn't."

"First," Cargill went on, "you demand to know the truth. Then you tell me to shut up. Well, you can't have it both ways, Alec. Which is it?"

"I didn't say that."

"Then I suggest you listen." But instead of going on,

172

Cargill turned and faced the window and looked out, humming softly to himself.

Infuriated, Alec decided simply to sit and wait. When Cargill wanted to talk, he would. Until then, patience would have to serve. Cargill could deliver him over to Ah Tran or any other messiah of his choice but that didn't mean he would cooperate. And he didn't intend to. He knew his own version of the truth, and that would have to serve him for now.

"I think we can beat them," Cargill said.

"What?"

Cargill shrugged and recommenced his melodic humming. Again, Alec restrained himself and was patient.

Finally, Cargill said, "I told you the truth before."

"Which time was that?" Alec asked, sarcastically.

"When I said I didn't kill her. She deserves more credit than that."

"If you didn't, who did? It wasn't me. I was out cold."

"I know. I knocked you out."

Cargill fell silent, either lost in thought or else pretending to be. The impenetrable density of his radiations did not change. Alec tried to remain patient but he couldn't do it any longer.

"Well, he said. "Which is it? Either you're going to tell me about Anna or you're not."

"I wish I could."

"What's stopping you."

Cargill glanced at the control panel, then shrugged. "Oh, nothing, I guess. But you must remember that I'm not a young man and, frankly, without going into details, women have long played a central role in my life. I have always attempted to know and, if and when possible, understand and sympathize with their race. It's hardly a simple process. Greater men than myself—I think of Tolstoy, Max Ophuls, Ibsen, Sternberg, Henry James—have tried and failed. Women are—to me—to us—an alien species. One might even say—with only a hint of facetiousness—that women were our first true supermen. I hope I'm not being pa-

173

tronizing when I say that I believe women—at their best—to possess all the worthier characteristics of men, plus several others that none of us will ever know. The point of all this—why I dare to bore you—is, of course, Anna. I want you to realize the significance of this remark: of all the women I have ever known or studied, she is the one I admire most."

"But you killed her."

"No," Cargill said. "I did not. I moved her body into the path of the flames in order to ensure that she received a fitting funeral. When I did that, she was already dead."

"That's impossible. Don't tell me there was someone else there."

"No."

"Well, then——"

For the first time, Cargill's radiations reached Alec clearly: anger.

"She killed herself, you idiot."

"Oh."

"I received a report that she had reached the city but, because of this stupid war and my visit to your office, it was delayed reaching me. Nevertheless, I rushed to your home immediately. As I wound my way up the path leading to your doorstep, I spied the flames. I ran ahead as if a demon were pursuing my tail and broke into the house. I went straight into the garden. Neither of you—clearly being involved in more private matters—detected my approach. I crept up behind you and delivered the necessary blow with a stick."

"But why me? You should have hit her."

"So that, in response, she would shoot you?" Cargill shook his head. "Besides, I would never strike a woman. I met Anna eye-to-eye. I started to speak, to voice a plea. It did not prove necessary. She simply turned the weapon on her own face and squeezed the trigger. It was over in a moment and she was dead. It was an act of divine sacrifice."

"Hardly." Alec laughed. "No one made her try to kill me."

174

Once more, Cargill's anger flared. He glared at Alec. "You call yourself a Superior. Think before you speak. Didn't you hear a word of what I told you before? She was under the control of her father, an Inheritor. He made her try to kill you."

"Then why didn't she?"

"A good question." Cargill nodded his appreciation. "But the answer should be obvious; Anna defied them. She asserted her humanity in what was, perhaps, the only way open to her: through suicide. Can you say the same?"

"You want me to kill myself?" Alec laughed.

"I want you to assert your own freedom. Other ways of doing so are open to you—they weren't for Anna."

"Such as?"

"Ah Tran and I will show you a way."

Alec said, "No," but this denial was by no means positive. What Anna had done—at least what Cargill claimed for her—could not fail to move him. She had sacrificed herself—in the face of dreadful odds—in order to save him. But why? What reason did she have for placing his life above her own? If he wished to lie, he could tell himself she had acted from motives of pure love. But he knew better: Anna hadn't loved him. Instead, he was beginning to understand that she had acted from more selfish motives. Anna had not saved him—no, she had saved herself. In dying, she had chosen to express her own freedom. And now Cargill wanted him to do the same. "All right, tell me what you want."

"I simply want you to agree to save yourself—and the world as well."

"You make that sound so simple. But how am I supposed to do it? By helping you and your friend, Ah Tran, I suppose. There's one thing wrong with that— Ah Tran is a fool. He—(Alec saw no point in continuing to conceal the truth)—doesn't understand reality. He tries to comprehend poetry through science. He tries to mix them together. He talks about souls in terms of ecosystems. That isn't just wrong—it's foolish."

"And why is that?" Cargill asked, evenly.

"Because when science and poetry are merged, the results are invariably a big mess." He gave Cargill some of the examples he had worked out for himself in the garden. Spoken aloud, the words somehow seemed less convincing but he refused to be diverted. "That's the way it is and not you or me or even Ah Tran can change it."

Cargill started to smile but clearly decided to suppress the reaction. He said, "You're wrong—there is no difference."

"Don't joke with me—please."

"I wouldn't, Alec, and I'm not."

"But don't you see? Science is concerned with the world as it is, while poetry conceives of an entirely different place, a world where things exist in the forms they ought to possess."

"But the world—this world—does exist in the form it ought to possess. Science merely confirms the inspirations of poetry, when those inspirations are valid. It has to be this way. In what other possible state could our world exist?"

"It isn't a place filled with love. It could be. It isn't beautiful or glorious or divine. It could be all of those. It could be a place without evil and ugliness and war and poverty and murder and hate and—"

"In other words," Cargill said, and he laughed, "it could be an incredible bore. What you're stating is an adolescent fantasy—a sterile view of a lifeless heaven. It could be as you say, but who really needs it?"

"Maybe I do—maybe the human race does."

"Then you'll have to do something about it, because I won't, but from what you say, you won't either."

"I've already found that world."

"And you won't let anyone else try?"

"Me?"

"Why not? Isn't that what Anna was trying to do?"

"I don't know. Anna is dead." Turning away from Cargill, Alec looked out the window and noticed that the plane was at last descending through the clouds. A sea of fluffy, unreal whiteness surrounded the plane.

"Let me explain," Cargill said. "I owe you that much." He told Alec about Ah Tran's experiments into the recreation of the mass racial consciousness of the species. "But, so far, he has always failed to reach his goal."

"I'm not surprised."

Then Cargill told about the circle of disciples, the spiritual conduit, and the death of Eathen.

Alec smiled on hearing the last. "So that's what you want from me. You tried to use one freak and he died and now you want to use another freak—me. Android or superman, they're both the same to you and your messiah. Less than human, so why not sacrifice them? Anna too. She's dead."

"She killed herself. To save you."

"To save herself."

"And you're afraid to do the same?"

"I don't need to."

"They are your fathers. Don't you owe the human race that much?"

"If the Inheritors are my fathers and the human race my mothers, why should I choose one over the other?"

"Anna did."

"Quit bringing her up. She failed."

"Are you sure?"

"Yes."

"Are you afraid?"

"Of what? Death? No—hardly."

"The war has already begun," Cargill said. "I'm afraid there's nothing any of us can do about that. But it will not last forever. Someday, the fighting will be done. What kind of world are we going to have then, Alec? Is it going to be the world as it ought to be? Who will rule? Who should? The decision is yours, Alec. Make your choice. The Inheritors? Or mankind?"

"So far man hasn't done so well. Maybe it's time to let someone else have a chance."

"Ah, you supermen," Cargill said, shaking his head. "Such a common error. Man has not failed. The fact is that he has, instead, succeeded quite gloriously. Your

177

view is limited only to those things that are wrong. You can see the war and privation, the killing and hate—but what about the successes, the accomplishments? You must realize that the human race is still barely in its childhood. Do we kill small boys because they have failed to accomplish adult aims? No. Don't we indeed allow these boys a chance to attain manhood, the opportunity to grow and develop and mature? What one boy is permitted, surely a whole race deserves as well."

The plane had pierced the layer of clouds. Alec looked down, seeing—without surprise—the vast blue wastes of the Pacific Ocean. From one side, a speck of land appeared, slowly expanding in size. Cargill took firm control of the plane. The land mass grew larger.

Alec was thinking. Everything Cargill had told him was, he knew, only an echo of phrases he had once uttered himself. For years, he had lectured the Superiors on the duty they owed the human race.

Had he come to reject all that? In the past few months, hadn't he experienced so much that the simple solutions of the past now seemed absurdly obsolete?

But Cargill had given him an opening. Anna. Hadn't she chosen to act not from motives of ideal selflessness but rather from an understandable need to express her own personal freedom? Could he do any less than that? Succeed or fail, didn't he owe himself that much?

Outside the window, a paved landing strip had materialized. The plane circled above. Cargill began to speak softly into the phone. The plane dipped, nose turned down, hurtling toward the earth below. A moment later, the wheels struck. The plane bounced, quivered, then rolled casually to a stop.

Alec turned and touched Cargill on the shoulder and said, in a rush, "All right—you win—I'm going to try it."

"I won?" Cargill asked.

A small crowd was rushing the plane. Among the mass, Alec recognized Ah Tran's familiar, worn features. He smiled. Right on time. Cargill had got it down to the last possible second. So that was the rea-

178

son for all those silly hesitations at the beginning of the voyage. Cargill didn't want Alec to have a chance to say no after he had once said yes. There was no time for changing his mind now.

"We both won," Alec said.

Cargill nodded and opened the door. He pointed at the crowd awaiting them.

"Let's go," he said.

twenty-four

Alec Richmond sat in the center of the circle.

What he wanted to do was ignore everything that existed outside or beyond the limits of his own self. It was not a simple process. There were twenty-four in the circle. Except for Ah Tran he knew none of them, who or what or why they were. Physically—and he turned his head to make sure—each seemed a rather insubstantial reflection of the person beside him. Whether male or female—and most were female— white or black—and only one was black—young or old—and only Ah Tran could be called old—such distinctions as these did not matter. Each of the disciples radiated a portion of himself, so that—in spite of his wishes—Alec could not keep them out entirely. After a time, he quit trying. It wasn't wholly necessary—not yet. He shouldn't deplete his strength too soon. The best way of handling the situation would be to wait for the mass to form, for the gestalt to be fused into a secure whole, and then, in a rush, he could easily obliterate that which was not relevant and then allow them (or it) to enter. What happened after that was more difficult to determine in advance.

He received snatches of information from around the circle. One of the women—barely a girl in fact—was anxious because, the night before, she had confessed to one of the men that she loved him and he had not, so far, chosen to make an answer. One man—for all Alec knew he might be the subject of the girl's concern—was

179

very upset because the wife he had deserted in London some months past had recently communicated a threat to have him confined to a mental home because, she claimed, his action in depositing their joint fortune in a Swiss bank account belonging to Ah Tran (under a phony name) indicated a certain looniness on the part of the man. All sorts of questions assailed him. Would the war intervene and prevent his wife from obtaining the court order she sought? Maybe, with luck, London would be the recipient of that now famous Indonesian A-bomb. Or should he take steps to free the money and see that his wife received a fair share, thus preserving his own freedom for the nonce? There was another young man, who wondered what position his father—the ruler of a primitive island kingdom unfortunately located less than a hundred miles from the center of civilized power—would take now that the war had actually begun. Would he (the father) feel it necessary, for reasons of national or personal pride, to field an army? And, if so, would he then consider it necessary to follow ancient tradition and recall his son and heir to head that army? As he sat in the circle, supposedly trying to meditate, the son struggled to recall some of the lessons he had been forced to study in early childhood relating to the tactical theories of battlefield action. If he was going to be a general, he had to know the proper way to fight.

Alec felt all of them—not just these three. The radiations reached him simultaneously but he had no difficulty separating one from the others. Never before had his talent come so near assuming the aspects of real telepathy. Although each of the disciples was striving to meditate, seeking to discover some abstract location upon which to focus all attention, none had as yet wholly succeeded and thoughts continued to flow. Alec saw anxiety, pleasure, guilt, jealousy, anger, bitterness, fear, envy, disgust, avarice, serenity, joy, pride, and loathing. Alec focused his attention on Ah Tran and although the messiah had withdrawn more fully than the others his thoughts were clearly open. Alec was surprised at what he discovered but not really shocked. He restrained himself to keep from laughing.

Alec realized it was time for him to act. Reaching out with his own mind, he sought to enter the others. He went to the young woman first and drove out all thoughts of her self-proclaimed future husband. He cautioned the man to forget his wife for the time being and further calmed the anxious recollections of the son and heir. He went to each of the twenty-four, smoothing out their psychic wrinkles, slicing off any jagged mental peaks, filling in the gaping chasms, creating a flat but equal wholeness.

Then he drew back. It was time for him to wait. Needing something to fill the gap, he recalled the ancient fable of the dying man and decided to try to review his own life. It was an easy process making it rise up. The events of a lifetime flowed neatly behind his eyes. He assumed an attitude of disinterested observation. He might have been watching one of Anna's more speculative sculptures. The life story of an incomplete superman. A tale without plot, theme, significance, or hero. The most valid artistic aspect of the tale was its keen ambiguity. What, he wondered, was the point? What about the author? Where did he stand in relation to his material? Artistic objectivity seemed quite total. Alec failed to detect, within the story, so much as a hint of tragedy, comedy, farce, allegory, or irony. The sequence of events proceeded casually from cause to effect. A child was born, placed in a home, because a man, married, worked, and—finally—riding in a small plane—turned to the pilot and said that yes, he would do it. Minor characters came and entered. Subplots flickered, then faded. At last, he saw himself seated within the circle. Was this the end? He couldn't tell but he stopped. Then he sat, witnessing what seemed to be an infinity of mirrors, endless dwindling layers of shining glass, one piled atop the other.

The twenty-four were gone. Instead, a single fused mass lay waiting. Alec trembled with sudden dread. Had he ever really expected this? They had succeeded. The mass beat against the hastily erected barriers of his mind, demanding entrance. For a time—involuntarily—he resisted.

Then he closed his mind, drawing back. It was too late now for saying no. He began to tear down his own self, moving through his mind from room to room, snuffing out an illumination he found. At last he came to a final lighted corner and, stopping here, he turned and raised the barriers, allowing the fused mass to rush through. It poured into his mind as thick as water, obliterating any final remnants of himself, drowning his soul, consuming him; and in the final flickering moments of his awareness, Alec reached out and grabbed the thing that had entered his mind and threw it high, like a rock, letting it soar upward and into the infinite unknown.

Then Alec Richmond was gone.

The fused spirit—departing the husk of the conduit—rose high. Propelled by the spark provided by the man once known as Alec Richmond, the mass sped into the heavens, reaching out, stretching toward a form of existence never previously known. The gestalt was whole now—fused and merged—and once it reached its proper dwelling place would assume a fixed location in the universe and be as truly and purely alive as any of its components once had been. Closer ... it came closer ... closer. The mass rushed through a world outside space, one lacking in color, light, and time. A place of utter nothingness and yet—near at hand—another place lay waiting, a world of synesthesia, where light was sound, color motion, and time space. The mass moved as an embryo now. Its existence seemed inexorable, as though firmly predestined, predicated upon events that had already occurred and could not be revoked.

But then the other thing came rushing down. In a flash of individual awareness, Alec knew: *Ford!* It came sweeping down—blackness—ripping · into the fused mass, lodging there, caught. The moment contact occurred, Alec screamed, *Father, father father*. He fought with all his might to drive this foul and ugly thing away. But he was burning up. As if he had been carried bodily through space and plunged into the heart of a flaming star. He could not fight. This thing was far stronger than himself. *Father, father, father.* The thing exuded an essence of such undiluted evil that Alec was suddenly certain that not only was there a Creator but a Destroyer and that this thing was as surely the son of the latter as Christ was born of God.

The thing of blackness permeated the fused gestalt. Alec glimpsed the dawning of his own end. He did struggle—yes—he resisted. But the barriers he erected to protect himself were as fruitless against this thing as the shield of a medieval knight raised against a cosmic bomb. The fusion began to shatter. Alec glimpsed them separately—the woman worried of her love, the heir and his father, the man and his wife, and even Ah Tran himself—rigid with fear. The broken gestalt limped through the summit of its arc, then turned downward. The earth rushed up, spinning, while Alec—alone—struggled to preserve some faint, lingering vision of life.

And then a flash of sudden whiteness swept over him and, with it, the sweeping pain was gone. A horrible weight was raised from his shoulders. The black thing was gone; the gestalt was set free. Quickly, though wounded, Alec struggled to fuse the mass together once more, to repair the injured fragments. He let it fall. The mass dipped, swung through the nadir of its arc, then soared high again. Alec died. He merged wholly with the mass. The place came near—land of synesthesia—paradise, heaven. It grew nearer. Closer. Closer. Close. . . .

And then it was there.

The journey was over.

The gestalt paused, trembling with eager expectation, but then, realizing that anticipation was no longer necessary, settled down to await the beginning.

And, soon enough, it came.

Later, Inspector Cargill approached the room where the circle had met. With the key Ah Tran had given him, he unlocked the door and peeped inside. He discovered the twenty-three remaining disciples, Ah Tran, and Alec Richmond seated exactly as he had originally left them. He shook his head, but without any real disappointment. In truth, he had not expected anything more. Ah Tran was his friend and an intelligent young man. Perhaps he had indeed stumbled upon some important spiritual technique and if that method had not proved great enough to save the human race, then the failure in itself could hardly be termed exceptional. After all, in all the past centuries of human life, no other method or technique had been invented, created, or detected capable, by itself, of providing complete spiritual salvation. Why should Ah Tran be allowed to succeed where so many others had failed before him? There was only one difference this time. Before, there had always been other times in which to try again. But the days were over now and, with them, the human race as well.

Cargill entered the room in order to find out exactly what had occurred. He approached the circle. The eyes of the disciples were shut. Only Alec, in the center, lifted his gaze as Cargill came near.

"What happened?" Cargill asked, standing behind the circle. "Are you all right?"

"Yes," Alec said, and his voice was barely more than a whisper.

The tone cause Cargill to shiver. "Don't tell me you—you made it?"

"Yes," Alec said. "We made it."

"We?"

"Yes. You see—" Alec smiled "—I am not I any more; I am we."

Cargill nodded. "I see."

Alec crooked a finger. "Come closer and we will tell you what happened."

"Yes, tell me," Cargill said, but he came no closer.

"We went up," Alec said, "just as you told me—told Alec. It was astonishing, the way we merged into a single glorious whole. We thought we would get there for certain this time. Then Ford came down. We tried to resist, but he was far too strong even for Alec. We

184

began to fall. Then, suddenly, Ford was gone. We returned and reached the place we sought. And that is where we are now."

"You killed him?"

"Ford? We do not know. Yes, perhaps that is what happened. But it did not seem that way. Perhaps we tired him and he was not able to fight us any more. But it did not seem that way either. He was gone and then we were there."

"But he isn't dead?"

Alec shrugged. "We can't know. Death is there and we are here." He giggled. "This is another universe."

"And I don't suppose you can tell me what it's like?"

"No, we cannot. But we are not alone here. There are other races here too. Other peoples who have achieved in the past what our race has achieved now."

"But you can't tell me any more?"

"You must come here first."

"How will I manage that?"

"We will assist you. All men must come here now that the path is open. We are a superman." Again, Alec giggled and stopped himself only by thrusting his fist into his mouth.

Cargill pretended not to notice. "Are you greater than the Inheritors?"

"The Inheritors, despite what they think, are merely the children of the human race. We are another, far superior race entirely."

"Then you can defeat them? Drive them away?"

"If necessary, that could be accomplished."

"If necessary? But I thought that was the whole point of this experiment."

"Their domain is limited to the Earth. Ours now spans the universe. They are harmless creatures now."

"What about Ah Tran?" Cargill pointed to one motionless figure within the circle. "I'd like to talk to him."

"Ah Tran no longer exists. He is part of us now."

"But I can talk to you, Alec."

"We are not Alec."

"Oh." Cargill stepped back, shaking his head. He glanced eagerly toward the door. "Is there anything you need? Food? Water? I can bring it."

"We need nothing."

"I see." Cargill stepped away. The eyes—Alec's eyes—followed him. He opened the door and slipped through. On the other side, alone again, he found he was shaking.

When he recovered, he threaded a path through the maze of floors and rooms and corridors and came at last to the kitchen, where he stopped to eat. He was munching on a sandwich when one wall of the room suddenly erupted in a blaze of light and sound and color. Dead-faced troops raced across a burnt and forsaken landscape.

The announcer's voice said, "An important victory was today attained by the civilized forces active upon the plains south of Manitoba. Western Hemispheric action has been declared inevitably successful. Current attack plans call for—"

Cargill realized he did not want to hear another word of this. What did it matter? The war was over and no one knew it yet but he. Searching the wall for some means of making the picture go away, he found nothing, finally giving up, kicking furiously out, thrusting the tip of his shoe through the center of the electronic battlefield. Obediently, the picture faded away.

Smiling, he went back to the sandwich. He thought, *He's gone mad,* and found the idea powerfully reassuring. He knew about reversion, how the Superiors, balanced precariously between two conflicting species, often fell into the chasm between. The pressure had got to Alec; he had gone mad.

But what about the others? The diciples? Ah Tran? Had Alec, in the end, proved strong enough to drag them down with him? Had his ravaged mind swallowed them up, consumed them too?

It was a frightening thought. But what was worse was the opposite. The human race saved and yet—he had to admit this—destroyed more utterly than the Inheritors could ever have hoped to accomplish. *If we have won*, he thought, *then what is wrong with me? Is it that I am merely me, myself, I? That I like to say I when I talk of me and never we or us or them? Is it that I am simply afraid?*

He looked down at himself, seeing the blue veins in his bare arms, the skinny legs, weak misshapen hips. He raised his hands and held them close to his face. *This is me*, he thought, *and I can never be we.*

He was mad. He had to be mad. The war would go on. In the end, they—the Inheritors—would win. The Earth was theirs. No one could stop them from claiming their prize.

He dropped his hands. *I am a man*, he thought and, thinking this, felt suddenly and awfully and dreadfully alone.

twenty-five

Henry J. McCoy was the sort of person who, when forced to go out unprotected on the streets, had to proceed in a sharp, cautious, constantly alert manner, for otherwise, if he wasn't careful, something big and strong and tough would surely pop up from someplace and run straight over him. The truth was that hardly anyone ever noticed the existence of McCoy. Even when he spoke forcefully and waved his hands and danced a vigorous jig, it was necessary to reassure passing strangers that this gesturing wraith was, in fact, something real.

McCoy was fully aware of these facts and took the necessary precautions. Years ago, when first contacted by the agents of Karlton Ford, he had tried in vain to convince them that they had the wrong man.

"You are Henry J. McCoy, born of unknown parentage in Oakville, Wisconsin, home patient number 4678-99-4744?"

"Well, yes, that's me," McCoy admitted.

"Then there can be no mistake. You are the man Mr. Ford wants." The agents had then proceeded to reveal that Karlton Ford had personally considered more than a thousand applicants for the position of his private secretary before eventually choosing McCoy.

"But I didn't apply," McCoy said.

"A personal application is not required. Mr. Ford considered the best men for the job and selected you." Salary would not be permitted to present any obstacle. McCoy could name his own price. All he had to do was agree to accept the work and promise to do the best job he knew how.

"I shouldn't but—" McCoy began. He made himself stop. Shouldn't? But why not?"

McCoy was then working for an old firm of corporate lawyers in San Francisco. He was chief clerk—the only clerk actually—but had already been notified that, come the new year, his position would be automated. More than a dozen times in the past, this same fate had overtaken McCoy. On one dreadful occasion, he had been forced to draw the government unemployment pension for more than a year. He had always flatly refused all offers of retraining. In spite of its precarious aspects, he loved his work. He was a clerk, which meant doing whatever his current employer ordered him to do. Invariably, he performed his assigned tasks in an efficient—if never brilliant—manner. He always worked twelve hours a day, seven days a week, and if he happened to complete all his assigned duties in less time than that, then he would immediately begin over again, hoping to achieve a nearer perfection the second time around. Outside of his job, he had one hobby, but that was not a time-consuming avocation and was perfectly respectable.

"All right," he said, shocking himself with the firmness of his tone. "I'll do it."

"There is one other requirement," the agents said. "You must divest yourself of all friends and close acquaintances. Mr. Ford demands that his employees devote all their available energies to him."

"Of course," said McCoy. And—no wonder: he didn't have a single friend and only a few, very vague acquaintances.

McCoy went to work for Karlton Ford the following week.

He occupied a modest room of his own at the Wyoming ranchhouse and was soon provided similar quarters in the various apartments around the world. Karlton Ford did not prove to be—in any conceivable way—a common or normal human being. But the work was good. Normally, McCoy labored sixteen hours a day, seven days a week, which left him time for seven good hours' sleep and one additional hour he could devote to his hobby.

That was collecting tape sculptures. Very respectable. Originals only. He experienced duplicates but would not collect them. No other form of art interested him in the least. He had never read a novel, studied a painting, heard a symphony, or seen a film. The hobby was his only eccentricity and as much as ninety percent of his salary was given over to new purchases. In fact, if it hadn't been for the hobby, he would gladly have been willing to work for board and room alone. But Karlton Ford paid splendid wages, and McCoy's collection grew to enormous proportions, threatening to spill both him and his small bed out into the corridor.

His favorite artist was a woman: Anna Richmond. Her work moved him in a way far deeper than mere words. She gave whatever meaning to his life that it possessed; and in return, well before he ever met her, Henry McCoy knew he must love her.

When she arrived at the ranchhouse, nothing about her changed his attitude. He liked to look at her—talking seemed less important—and so, though never neglecting his assigned duties, he often crept to some place where he might observe her without being seen in return. A dirty window. An untrimmed hedge. A broken fence. A stray hole in a wall. He felt a need to reconcile the mortal, flesh and blood visage of Anna with the divine inspiration that flowed through her work. McCoy acted no differently than any small boy suddenly confronted by the image of his ideal hero.

Then one night Anna went away on a plane programmed to carry her to San Francisco. McCoy placed her on board himself but she wouldn't answer the frantic questions he put to her.

Late the following day, Karlton Ford called McCoy to the sunporch on the roof and told him to take a letter. McCoy was so worried about Anna that it wasn't until the third paragraph that he realized what the letter was about.

"No!"McCoy cried, dropping pen and paper. "What are you talking about? Anna? Dead? No!"

Ford glared angrily. "She tried to murder her husband. The police shot her down."

"But she loved him."

"Her husband? Don't be—"

"I know she did. She told me—told him. I heard her talking to herself."

"Well, next time—" Ford showed his impatience "—don't listen."

McCoy sprang to his feet and pointed an accusatory finger: "You—you killed her!"

Ford blinked, astonished. "What did you say to me?"

McCoy waved the finger. "I know you, Mr. Ford. You think you can make anyone do whatever you want. Anna was your daughter but you treated her like dirt—you never loved her. I could tell. You did things to her mind. You made her into a zombie. You're a monster! Monster! Monster! You killed her and now—!"

Ford's face flushed with anger. As he spoke, McCoy felt the first tentative hints of some painful presence encroaching on his mind. But he went on, rushing desperately to finish, wanting to say what he had to say before he was struck down.

Then Ford fell back. His face lost its angry expression. The painful presence disappeared from McCoy's mind.

"McCoy," said Ford, very softly, as if from far away. "You may go away. I won't need you here any more." His eyes dropped shut; he seemed to drift away.

McCoy had seen this happen often enough before.

Standing, he left Ford as he lay. He went to the elevator and rode it down into the house. He passed through the kitchen.

Here, without intending to, he stopped. He leaned against a wall, clenched his fists tightly, and began to weep and wail. It wasn't the Anna Richmond he had known here for whom he cried; it was the work. He remembered all the titles and each one meant something deep and warm and significant. There was *Last Woman* and *Passion, Tomorrow's Children, Tenderness, Crime and Punishment, Gloria.* Only three days before, he had managed to acquire the original copy of her latest piece, *New Messiah,* the one about the android. Now none would follow. Anna Richmond was dead and that meant her work must be buried with her.

"You!" he cried, slamming his fists against the wall like a man deprived of the one firm, meaningful aspect of his entire existence. "You! You! You!"

On the kitchen table, something caught the light and glinted. He went over and raised the butcher knife in his hands. The blade was long, bright, and silver.

He rushed back to the sunporch.

Ford was lying on his back. His eyes were open but unseeing. His face and forehead were wrinkled, and his body was covered with a coating of sweat. The muscles in his legs and arms and neck were tensed and rigid as though engaged in some mighty, internal struggle.

McCoy noticed none of this. All he saw was Karlton Ford—Ford, the murderer—open and vulnerable.

McCoy raised the glinting knife and brought it straight down. The blade plunged through Ford's bare chest and penetrated his heart.

He died at once.

McCoy then left the blade where it was and hurried downstairs. He called the local police and explained what had happened but they were late in coming and when they did arrive refused to believe his story until he took them up on the roof and showed them the body.

"Good Lord, why?" asked one of the detectives. "Didn't you have a reason?"

McCoy made one attempt to express his feelings, but there was simply no way of communicating such intricate and sensitive motives. He fell into a sullen silence.

The detective shook his head wearily. "I'm so sick of this. I've never seen a murder that made any sense at all. What's supposed to be gained? What's ever changed or made over or made better or made right? It's not just stupid—it's pointless."

Overhead, a rocketplane blasted the silence of late afternoon and McCoy could not reply.